Narrow Road

DOM CONTRERAS

WORKBOOK PRESS LLC
187 E Warm Springs Rd,
Suite B285, Las Vegas, NV 89119, USA

Website: https://workbookpress.com/
Hotline: 1-888-818-4856
Email: admin@workbookpress.com

Ordering Information:
Quantity sales. Special discounts are available on quantity purchases by corporations, associations, and others. For details, contact the publisher at the address above.

Library of Congress Control Number:
ISBN-13:   000-0-00000-000-0 (Paperback Version)
                000-0-00000-000-0 (Digital Version)

REV. DATE: 10/17/2022

THE NARROW ROAD

"For the gate is small and the way is narrow that leads to life, and there are few who find it." Matthew 7:14 (NASB)

By: Dr. Dom Contreras Ph.D.

TABLE OF CONTENTS

Prologue...i

CHAPTER 1..1

CHAPTER 2...9

CHAPTER 3..25

CHAPTER 4..31

CHAPTER 5..48

CHAPTER 6..61

CHAPTER 7..74

CHAPTER 8..84

CHAPTER 9..86

CHAPTER 10...107

CHAPTER 11...115

CHAPTER 12...134

CHAPTER 13...155

CHAPTER 14...167

CHAPTER 15...182

CHAPTER 16...215

CHAPTER 17...231

CHAPTER 18...250

Epilogue..256

Prologue

The Narrow Road is a fictional story about a preacher who winds up in the town of Cambria California in 1928, after working for a few years with the migrant field workers. He is part Spanish and part Irish. He is almost broke financially, and when he arrives in town, he stops in one of the few restaurants in the ocean community. He starts his journey by working as a dish washer then is asked to be their minister. Unbeknown to the congregation, he is on a mission to get the church to see how far they have sinned by rejecting God's laws. He does amazing things in the name of the Lord, has a compassionate way with the people coming to grips with their sins, and repent for forgiveness before God.

The year 1928 was the year before the Great Depression. This came the following year. But when he arrived in town, where moon shine whiskey was sold along with bootleg whiskey, a murder is committed to cover up all that is going on in the community and affecting the church.

All the characters in this story are fictional, but the acts that the Preacher performs are Biblical.

What I have written as to some of the illegal acts committed by the church have been done in a handful of ministries.

I dedicate this book to all the minister throughout our country that are struggling to get their church to be like Christ intended to, and can be mighty tempting to a young minister or a veteran minister who has struggled, monetarily; the tempter is at the door, waiting to devour you.

[32] "Now I commit you to God and to the word of his grace, which can build you up and give you an inheritance among all those who are sanctified. [33] I have not coveted anyone's silver or gold or clothing. [34] You yourselves know that these hands of mine have supplied my own needs and the needs of my companions. [35] In everything I did, I showed you that by this kind of hard work we must help the weak, remembering the words the Lord Jesus himself said: "It is more blessed to give than to receive." (Acts 19:32-35 NIV)

All scripture is KJV unless otherwise stated by author.

CHAPTER 1

It was exceptionally warm for a late spring day. The Preacher chugged along in his Model T Ford. He had to change lanes in order to go West onto a bumpy road to the coast. He wondered, *why the road was so rocky and winding?* He so engrossed in his thoughts, when he abruptly swerved the automobile to avert hitting a small animal. He stopped and looked down at his feet, and there was a little dog. It was not a mongrel breed, but a Jack Russell Terrier. The Preacher picked the dog up and held him in his arms, speaking kind words to his newfound companion. He pulled over to the side of the road and looked at his little map that he had on his lap. As he looked closer at the map, he noticed that he was a few miles from the coastline of California, near a small community called Cambria.

Cambria, in those days, was a very small community with one gas station, a small hotel, one or two small restaurants, and a handful of residents. As he drove into the town, he pulled over to the side of the road in front of a small coffee shop, turned the engine off, and got out of the car with his little partner. He found a piece of rope in the car and tied the little fella to the bumper. He opened the door and walked over to the counter, and sat down in a wobbly stool. He thought, *I hope I have enough money to pay for this meal*, as he glanced at the menu and searched for the price of a bowl of stew and a cup of coffee. He had to be very careful with his finances since he had left Texas with only about $50.

While on his way to Cambria, he stopped at various farms and worked alongside with the itinerant farmers for a dollar a day. He glanced up and saw a tall, slender woman whom he assumed was the waitress. To him, she was very attractive with dark blue eyes and a creamy white skin. Her hair was jet black like a raven as the sun shines on its feathers.

The first words out of her mouth were, "What can I do for you.?"

He smiled and said, "I'll have a bowl of your stew and a cup of black coffee."

The waitress smiled and said, "Are you looking for work? I need a dishwasher. Mine didn't show up today. From the looks of your car, if that is what you call it, I do not know where you came from, but I am sure you had to stop a lot of times due to the age and the model. From the sound of the engine, it's not in very good shape. I'll pay you 25 cents an hour for a couple of days, if you are interested. I also have a little room in the back where you can sleep.

How's that sound to you?"

He answered, "It's a kind offer, but let me think about it."

The Preacher looked around the little coffee shop as he thought to himself, *maybe you could seat forty people with the six little tables and the twelve stools.* He was startled, when the waitress returned with a plate of hot stew along with a cup of coffee.

"Mister, I normally do not offer jobs to strangers, but there is something about you that makes me feel happy inside. You are a preacher, am I right? There is also a room in back with a cot, all you can eat, and a place where your dog can stay.

"Miss, you are the best thing that has happened to me in quite a long time. I have been on the road for almost a year. I spent some time in a small town in Texas as the Preacher of a Methodist Church. Most of the places that I have been in think I am a fraud because as an itinerant minister, I travel all the time. One day, while driving to a field to work, a child ran out in front of me, and of course, he was killed on impact. I started drinking as I blamed myself. One day, I awoke lying in the gutter with the rain pouring down on me. It hit me like a ton of bricks as I realized I had turned my back on my God, the Lord Jesus Christ. Looking back, I think he allowed me to go through my trials so that in the future, I would be a better witness for Him. The Bible teaches us that our trials strengthen our faith, so we in turn can help others who are going through difficult times."

"When I saw you get out of your car, I knew that you are a preacher. I lost my husband over in France in 1918, and left me with two little two-year-old twin boys. I have had to be the mother and father to the two of them, especially at night when they ask me as to when their daddy is coming home. I feel I am bursting at the seams as I try to hold back my tears."

He said, "I am so sorry you feel that way. Can I pray for you?"

"Please, Preacher; it would be a blessing. I feel better already just talking to you."

He took her arm, held her hand, and said a prayer of emotional healing. He added a verse of Scripture found in 2Corinthians (1:3KJV) "Blessed *be* God, even the Father of our Lord Jesus Christ, the Father of mercies, and the God of all comfort."

The Preacher stood up and said, "God bless you, daughter. From now on, you will feel His presence in your heart in a special way." He started to say something when she turned and saw the clock on the wall as it struck three times.

She said, "Oh, my! Look at the clock. It's time to get ready for our evening customers. What do they call you or what is your name?"

"My name is Leonardo Flynn. My father was Irish, and my mother was Spanish. My mother's name was Leanora, so I am named after my mother, but you can call me Len, or Preacher."

"Okay, Preacher. Before you go and tackle the kitchen, you better get your little dog and feed him some scraps and some fresh water. I saw him jumping up and down trying to get loose."

He said, "Okay, but Miss… uh… what can I call you?"

"My name is Deborah, but my friends call me Deb. My last name is Johnsen. I have a twin sons called Thomas and Paul, nine years old. My parents' names are Eric Swensen, but goes by the name of Swede. Mum's name is Clarise, and likes to be called Clare or Mother Swensen."

He said, "Miss Johnsen, let me go get the little feller before he strangles himself." He ran outside to the curb and reached down and hugged him as Little Feller. The Preacher said, "Little Feller, from now on, is your name." Little Feller continued licking his face. "Look Feller, I have a stack of pots and pans that need looking after." He no sooner got the words out of his mouth when the people started coming in and found their favorite table. He could see the people rushing to get their orders in. By this time, the evening waitress came in. She was a large woman and looked like she had experienced a rough life. She carried herself well in a defiant way, yet when she articulated, she had a way of being joyful. She said her name was Candice, but preferred to be called Candy.

The main menu was a weekly special: Prime Rib for $1.35 with drink included until sold out. Deb couldn't keep up with the demand until she ran out of Prime Rib. The sign said no substitutes. The Preacher had to work extra hard to keep up with the orders as he looked at the clock as it said 8:45 PM. Around nine thirty, he glanced through the small window into the dining area and noticed how fast the crowd had cleared out. Before he knew it, there walked in five men and sat down at one of the tables. The one who came in first sat at the head of one of the tables. They all looked at each other, and then got up and walked into the side room. The Preacher knew that the men were the church deacon board.

Deborah broke his silence and said, "The meeting of the church board is about to start. You can quit for the night. I'll see you in the morning."

"Great," he said. "Wait a minute. I need to know a few things so I can plan my time. First, what time do you want me here in the morning and what time do you open? Second, what hours do you want me to work and what day do I have off, and if I'm going to be here more than this weekend."

She responded, "First, we open at seven so I need you here 'till lunch time. During the week, we are busy in the morning. We start again at five 'till around eight. Sometimes, I close at eight but my sign says open from seven 'till nine. This week is Founder's Week, so on Saturday, we close early. We are closed Sunday through Monday, and during bad weather, we open and close early depending on the road conditions. We rarely have to close, but we hope we will grow in size when the railroad comes. The mines played out, so most of our busy time is during harvest time. Along with the beach crowd, they rent small cabins North of here along the beach. Hope this answers your questions."

The Preacher said, "It sure does but who feeds the five in the small meeting room?"

Deborah answered, "I make coffee for the men. Sometimes, the meetings go clear into the next morning, and if they want anything, they prepare it. Good night! See you in the morning. Hope and pray that things will work out for you. I pray to God that the board will hire you as minister of our small church. Again, good night! See you in the morning."

He said, "I will remember you in my prayers, Deborah. One of my prayers is that your mind will be at ease because God has it all planned. Amen!"

He shuffled off to his room in the back of the restaurant. Little-Feller was sleeping on the cot. As soon as he entered the room, the dog jumped up into his lap. He was pretty tired since he had put in a long day washing dishes. It is not an easy chore in a small restaurant because you have to do them by hand. In a modern restaurant, they use steam cleaners to wash them. He laid down and that is all he remembered as he went to sleep with Little Feller sleeping next to him.

CHAPTER 2

The Preacher was startled as he jumped out of bed thinking *where am I*, then he realized where he was. He looked out the window to see Deborah alighting from her car, as the clock said 6 AM. It was time to get up and for him to do his morning devotionals. He read a passage from the Book of Psalms then he started his prayers.

Morning was his favorite time because it meant that he could spend time with the Lord. He heard a knock on the door and he said, "Come in." He noticed it was Deborah with a hot cup of coffee and a couple of donuts.

Deborah said, "You can have a full lunch to make up for the small breakfast, if that is okay with you."

He said, "I generally do not eat breakfast, but these two donuts and a good hot cup of coffee always hits the spot." He asked Deborah, "What time did the meeting break up?"

"I do not know. I am not part of the board and my father is also one of the board members. He is part owner of this restaurant so he has access to anything he wants."

The Preacher said, "I slept like a baby, I didn't hear

them leave."

The Preacher and Deborah finished their breakfast, then went to work. The day went by rapidly. The Preacher worked hard. It has been sometime since he had worked so hard. In the late evening, the dinner crowd was still eating.

Deborah said, "I have invited a couple of board members to meet you, if that's okay with you."

He answered, "Of course, it is."

She no sooner got the words out of her mouth when in walked her father along with one of the other board members. Deborah introduced the Preacher to her father and to the other gentleman, Mr. Cartwright, who was one of the area's largest growers. Swede motioned to Deborah and the Preacher to take a seat in one of the small tables near the window.

While the Preacher chatted with her father and Mr. Cartwright, Deborah looked at the clock and said, "Gentleman, I must leave you due to the time. It is almost 7 o'clock and my early dinner people will start coming in for their meals. You gentlemen can continue talking since I have a feeling it is about selecting a new minister for the church."

They decided that it was better for them to meet in the back room. They went to the back room with a cup of coffee in their hands. Swede sat down at one of the tables and Cartwright sat next to Swede. The Preacher sat across from them.

Swede spoke up and said, "I suppose, Preacher, you are wondering what we wanted to talk to you about. It has to do with the minister vacancy. We have need of a minister since our old minister resigned for personal reasons. It will only be Brother Cartwright and myself tonight. We are the membership committee, looking for a man of God, who is a man of integrity. My question to you is, are you interested in the position?"

The Preacher answered, "Gentleman, I am flattered that you would ask me to such a high position, a complete stranger to you. Before we go any further in our dialog. I pray for God's blessing on our discussion, especially when I am going to make an important decision. I pray wisdom in how God wants me to respond to your question. If you do not mind, I would like to pray right now that our conversation would glorify our Lord and Savior Jesus Christ, if this meets with your approval."

Both Swede and the other board member, Jake Cartwright, in unison said, "Of course, we want to pray and believe that the word of God says, all things should be prayed for. Jake, would you lead us in prayer?"

After they prayed for guidance and direction for the

church, that they would make a proper decision in choosing a new minister, and welcomed the opportunity to talk to the Preacher, Jake asked the questions when interviewing a candidate for such a responsible position. He asked questions about family, marriage, children, his education, especially the seminary or Bible college that he graduated from.

The Preacher said, "Gentleman, why don't you let me give you a brief rundown on my education and my family life, if that is okay with you."

Both men agreed without hesitation.

"Preacher, what is your last name?"

"My last name is Flynn, and my first name is Leonardo; Len for short. My mother was Spanish and Native American. I had two sons, and a wife. They all died of the Spanish flu a few years ago. I was ordained by the Methodist denomination almost 20 years ago, and went to a seminary in Texas. I do not have any living relatives except one aunt who lives in Rio Oso, Texas, a small town near the border between Mexico and the United States. This is the only place I call home. When my wife and sons died, I went and stayed with my aunt for a short time. I wanted to die, so I took to drinking. Until one morning with the rain falling and hitting my face, I found myself lying in the gutter. Forgive me if I get emotional. It's due to the encounter I had with the Lord. Please let me continue. As I was saying, I had completely turned my back on my God. I left my church that I oversaw for almost 20 years as minster. I bummed around working in the fields picking cotton doing seasonal work mainly with Hispanics. Since I spoke the language, I was able to witness to them about the good Lord. At night, we would sit around the campfire singing Spanish songs along with Christian songs as well. I learned what Christian humility is. Being humble is something we have to search for as we examine our own hearts. The last two years of my life are very precious because of what I learned from working with hard-working field hands. I felt God wanted me to come out West. The Holy Spirit guided me to Cambria. My quest came to an end when I stopped and picked up a little stray dog. He was a gift from our Lord. I drove into your little town, thinking perhaps I could fill the void that I felt in my spirit. I heard that little voice inside saying to me, *this is where I want you to be.* I never dreamed that my quest would open a door for me to minister to God's people in this small community. Let me say a few things about my needs. First and foremost, I am not in the ministry to make money. I chose the ministry because I wanted to serve God's creation. His written word states that He will supply all my needs not my wants. I have only one request from you, I ask of you that you would let me try out for a couple of Sundays, if that is suitable for the committee and the board members. I will be ready this Sunday if that meets with your approval."

Swede and Mr. Cartwright looked at each other and said, "Certainly! We look forward to your sermon. Would you mind giving us a background of the town and the board members in your previous church so that we can have your resume on file. If there are any more questions, you need to ask us. Now's the time, Reverend."

"No, I don't."

"I see you don't have any more questions so we will say good night to you. Please lead us in a closing prayer, Reverend. Until the day after tomorrow is Sunday. Oh, we almost forgot, we gather as a board each Sunday morning a half-hour before services, to pray for the congregation and the message that you will bring."

They both got up and started for the door and left. The Preacher went into the kitchen to wash some of the dishes left from the current day. He went to bed and slept soundly until he awoke by the sounds he heard in the kitchen. He went to the kitchen and saw it was Deborah.

Deborah came into the kitchen as she was preparing a breakfast of ham, eggs, and toast for the Preacher. She stopped next to the sink where he was starting to wash the dishes, and asked, "How did it go last night?"

He answered, "It went well. I will bring God's word to the congregation this Sunday. The board members were nice enough to listen to my testimony. I know they felt the love of God in me by their reactions. Today is Saturday and I suppose it will be a very busy since it is Founder's Day, then tomorrow is Sunday. I look forward to meeting some of the parishioners. I want to thank you personally for seeing something in me that was worth saving."

Deborah said, "I meant what I said with all my heart. You are a shining light to my soul. I will cherish this encounter the rest of my life."

"Thank you again, Deborah, for being there for me as well."

"Oh, my!" he said. "Look at the clock; it says seven thirty." As he spoke, customers started coming into the restaurant, and of course, they were chatting about what was coming up tonight. There was a social gathering at the school gymnasium starting at 8 o'clock. All were invited to their annual Founder's Day's festivities, and no alcohol allowed. He thought to himself *I might drop by for a short while, depending on how tired I was.*

The morning seemed to fly by as the Preacher glanced at the clock and saw it was 10:30 AM. The breakfast crowd was gone. Deborah called the Preacher to come over and take a break. He made his way to one of the tables where

Deborah was sitting, sipping a hot cup of coffee. He sat down with his cup of coffee, as she said, "How do you feel after a busy morning doing dishes?"

The Preacher responded by saying, "I feel pretty good about the work I had to do this morning."

Deborah said, "It can sure get hectic around here, especially when people get agitated if they do not receive their food right on time, as if there was a time when you are not busy."

The Preacher said, "Deborah, it has been a long time since I felt good about washing dishes along with pots and pans. As I worked, I reflected on the conversation I had with you and the board members. I must say it was all an answer to prayers. I am sure I won't please everybody. If I am accepted as your Minister, there are always those who doubt the other members for the selection they made. There is not much choice for a church in a small community. I came here at the right time. I would like to know; how many other churches are there in this little town?"

Deborah thought a minute, then said, "I think there are two other Protestant churches, one at the edge of town. Another one that meets at the grade school, but I am told that the one that meets in the school is small since they barely take in enough money to pay for the rent, let alone a Minister's salary. There is also a Roman Catholic church at the end of town that has been there for many years. In fact, it is said that the Catholic Church was founded shortly after the founding of our community. Oh, and the Orthodox congregation meets in the Grange. The Franciscan fathers brought the message of the gospel to the Native Americans that lived in this area. We are not at war with other denominations. Christ our Savior stated as part of his message was unity."

"You are right, Deborah. Paul the Apostle stated in Ephesians 4:12 (KJV), "And he gave some apostles; and some prophets; and some, evangelists; and some, pastors and teachers; For the perfecting of the saints, for the work of the ministry, for the edifying of the body of Christ: Till we all come in the unity of the faith, and of the knowledge of the Son of God, unto a perfect man, unto the measure of the stature of the fullness of Christ: That we *henceforth* be no more children, tossed to and for, and carried about with every wind of doctrine, by the sleight of men, *and* cunning craftiness, whereby they lie in wait to deceive; But speaking the truth in love, may grow up into him in all things, which is the head, *even* Christ: From whom the whole body fitly joined together and compacted by that which every joint supplieth, according to the effectual working in the measure of every part, maketh increase of the body unto the edifying of itself in love." The Preacher continued to speak of the unity needed in the church. He said, "That he felt that the church somewhere along the way forgot that apostles, prophets, evangelist, pastor and teachers are to teach and instruct the church to prepare them to fulfill the words of our Lord, "And Jesus came and spoke unto them, saying, all power is given unto me in heaven and in earth. Go ye therefore, and teach all nations, baptizing them in the name of the Father, and of the Son, and of the Holy Ghost: Teaching them to observe all things whatsoever I have commanded you: and, lo, I am with you always, *even* unto the end of the world. Amen." Matthew 28:18-20 (KJV). Forgive me, Deborah, do you mind if I use your full name? I find Deborah such a beautiful name and I feel more comfortable, if it's okay with you." By the look in her eyes, the Preacher knew that it was all right. He sensed that her deceased husband was the only one she would allow to address her as Deborah, a sign of their love between them. The Preacher said," Deborah's name is mentioned in the Bible, the book of Genesis and Judges. The Genesis account tells us she was Rebekah's maid and died on Jacob's journey back to Canaan. There was also Deborah, the prophetess, who judged Israel in the time of the Judges."

They were both startled when a large group of young people came into the coffee shop. They were very loud and unruly and demanded service immediately.

The Preacher stood up and looked at them with his penetrating eyes that spoke his authority. He said, "If you act like children, expect to be treated as such. This lady will take your orders, but you must adhere to the sign. We have the right to refuse service to whom we choose. It seems to me that you are starting to celebrate Founder's Day early. Corn liquor or moonshine is against the law. We are law abiding citizens. Start behaving like adults or you can leave… now!"

A tall lanky fellow who seemed to be the leader of the pack, said, "Who do you think you are, old man? You act like you're the owner of this greasy spoon. What are you going to do about your archaic rule? Fight us all?"

The Preacher stood up instinctively grabbed the young man by his arms and pulled him to the entrance. He grabbed him by his britches and tossed him out into the street. He looked around at a burly-looking male who started to jump him, but he was quicker on his feet than he was. Another one lunged at him, but within an instant he subdued them both, and sent them running out the door. He said, "Remember; the good book says: 'it is more blessed to give than to receive' (Acts 20:35 KJV)." He turned and saw a couple of what was left of their gang who came over and said they were sorry for their actions.

The Preacher said, "I humbly accept your apology.

Deborah please give these two young men and these young ladies a hamburger and soda on me. By the way, are you folks from around here? If you are, you are welcome to come to church in the morning. Be there at ten, okay? Also, I'll see you tonight at the social. Remember, no alcohol is allowed."

By this time there were other customers coming into the restaurant.

Deborah decided to close at 4:00pm so they could clean early and have time to rest up for the social which was set to start at eight. The afternoon customers stopped coming in at around 3 o'clock. Deborah went over and closed the front door, placed her sign that said, *'Closed for the rest of the day.'*

Deborah turned around and said to the Preacher, "There is time for us to clean the kitchen and mop the floors as well as washing the dishes, pots and pans. When we open Tuesday morning, we will be ready."

When he looked at the clock, it said 5:45 PM. He had dried the last pot as he wiped his brow. He called out to Deborah as she was finishing mopping the floor in the restaurant.

He said, "it looks like we are all done. Deborah, you look tired and worn out; are you sure you will be ready to go to the festival tonight?"

She responded, "I certainly will be after I take a

good hot bath and get some of this perspiration off my body. Preacher, if you want to take a bath or shower, you can go to the parsonage. There are plenty of soap and hot water, and of course, towels. I was wondering if you had a clean shirt. If you don't, I have a few things that belonged to my husband. I am afraid that his suit would be too short in the pants but, there is a nice sports jacket that you can wear with your suit pants. Perhaps if you leave early from the festivities, it will give you enough time to prepare your message for the church in the morning. Does that sound okay to you?"

He answered, "It certainly is a good plan and we will stick by it. I always spend time late into the evening when I am preparing a sermon for the following day. Normally, I would start preparing at the beginning of the week for the following Sunday service. I think we should close up and start getting ready for the evening festivities."

Deborah agreed, "Let's go."

The Preacher went directly to the back room to check and see Little Feller. He decided to take him for a short walk. He did not know the streets at all. He glanced up and down as to which way to go. He decided to go North on the street in front of the restaurant. He noticed that the sign said 'Main Street'. He did not walk very far but noticing some of the buildings that were empty or at one time before the great fire, which burned many of the older homes and buildings. There were signs of this where you could see some of the outline of foundations where a building once stood.

At one time, Cambria had been a thriving community due to the quicksilver mine in the area until it ran out. The early settlers were Italian-Swiss, who settled in the area which brought in produce farmers as it stands today. The earliest settlers who founded the community were the Franciscan Fathers. He was so engrossed in his thoughts when all of a sudden, a car pulled over in front of him and blocked his passage.

Two men jumped out of the car and said to him, "Are you the fellow who abused our boys?"

The Preacher said, "You are mistaken. I defended myself and disciplined your boys. It shows very clear the way they act that they do not have much guidance or discipline at home. Since it looks like you are set on punishing me for the things your sons tried to do to me, you need Christ in your lives."

About this time, one of the two men lunged at him, but the Preacher was too quick with his feet as he caught the first man's hand and blocked the blow.

The other fellow looked at him and said, "Mister, I do not want any part of you. I think we took on more than we could handle, and besides, I did not know that you are a Preacher."

The man looked over to where his partner was stretched out on the ground, moaning about what the Preacher had done to him. He went over to the car, and pulled out a canteen full of water and poured it on his partner. He slowly got up and said to the Preacher, "Mister, where did you learn to fight like that?"

The Preacher responded by saying, "I was heavyweight champion of my class in college. My father was a professional boxer and he taught me how to defend myself. I am sorry but I believe that your sons need to learn Godly discipline. Tomorrow would be a good time to start by coming to our church at 10 o'clock. I hope to see you both with your sons. Oh, before I forget, we are having our Founder's Day celebration at the high school gym. Maybe I will see you there. One more thing, you know that alcohol in any form you drink is prohibited by law. I do not want to see anyone inebriated. You can eat all sorts of foods and deserts that the ladies have prepared, along with square dancing and socialize with other people. If you have a Bible, you need to read Ephesians 6:1-6. Hope to see you on Sunday."

The two men left in their car as the Preacher walked back to his room at the rear of the restaurant. He glanced at the clock, and it was a little after seven. He decided to rush over to the parsonage and take a quick bath. As he dried off with a couple of bath towels, he noticed clean underwear neatly placed on the bed and a clean shirt that he could wear for the evening. He also took out of his suitcase, a black suit that needed brushing off with a cloth brush. He was glad that he had one. He put on his suit and brushed it until he got rid of the dust and wiped a portion of the pants that had a few small food spots. He looked in the mirror in the bedroom to see how he looked. He felt he would pass inspection with a clean shirt Deborah had loaned him. He finished dressing as he picked up his Bible and Little Feller, and walked back to the restaurant, then went to school.

The Preacher decided to walk to the school which was about three city blocks. It was a cool evening as he felt comfortable walking with the breeze gently cooling his face. He had an old pocket watch that his father had left him, most of the time it didn't keep good time. He looked at the time, which said it was 8 o'clock, it would take about 10 minutes to his destination. His thoughts went back and forth to when he first came into town a couple of days ago. He was reminded of what he thought about this new town in which he would bring the word of God. He looked up as he arrived at the high school gym. He could hear the music and the type of dancing. They were square dancing. He took a deep breath and walked into the auditorium not knowing what to expect.

CHAPTER 3

As soon as he walked into the auditorium, Deborah came over and approached the Preacher with an older woman, "Reverend, I want to introduce you to one who has been anxious to meet you."

The Preacher knew that it was Deborah's mother. In fact, Deborah was a carbon copy of her mother.

Deborah said, "Reverend, this is my mother Mrs. Swenson."

"It is my pleasure," said the Preacher.

"Sir You can call me Mother Swenson, but my name is Clare. It's an honor to meet a minister of the Gospel. Deborah has not stopped talking about you since you came into the restaurant. I hope you decide to stay here. We are starting a lodge not too far from here. We feel that the town will start growing once the railroad is complete. Someday, the highway between us and Paso Robles will be paved so that travelers can come and stay at the Lodge. I welcome you in behalf of all the families in our community, and especially the ones who are here tonight. As you can see, most of the people are having a great time. Oh before I forget, forgive me for not greeting you with a dish of all sorts of appetizers."

The Preacher responded by saying, "It is an honor to be here. I firmly believe that the good Lord led me to your town. The Lord guided me here as He directed Abraham. I look forward to meeting all of the ladies and men in the church as well, along with some of the town's people. As you know, I will be preaching in the morning. I am excited to share with you what God has placed on my heart." As he finished his sentence, Deborah's father came over and welcomed him as well.

The caller called out that the next dance would be the Virginia Reel. The Preacher looked at Deborah and asked her to dance with him. Of course, she accepted as they walked to the dance floor where the people were lining up with their partners. All the people who were in attendance at the festivities were laughing and singing and some were standing around talking with old friends and new friends. The Preacher thought it will be nice to work together, doing the Lord's work. Being part of a larger family, serving each other and sharing their lives with Him. Perhaps they will start to work together in unity as the Lord commands. He thought of (Psalm 133:1 KJV) that stated, 'How good and how pleasant it is for the brethren to dwell together in unity.'

The Preacher looked at the large clock on the wall

and thought to himself, *where did the time go to.* He was having so much fun folk dancing. It had been years since he had had so much fun. He pulled Deborah over to one side of the dance hall and said to her that he was leaving and would see her in the morning.

He said, "I have to leave and prepare my sermon for tomorrow morning. I had a great time. Hope to see a few more Founder's Days in the future. God bless you and I will remember you in my prayers tonight." He walked out into the night air and looked up at the sky at all the stars as they glittered like diamonds. On top of that, it was a full moon. As he took in the smell of fresh air, he noticed a small taint of salt air. He thought it makes sense, since we are about a mile from the ocean. He decided that tomorrow, he would take Little Feller for a walk along the oceanfront.

As he neared the backroom of the restaurant, he noticed a slender figure of a woman, all dressed in white as she turned to walk into the woods, then disappeared. He would have to inquire about the apparition he had seen, then decided not to say anything as he opened the door and lit the kerosene lamp next to his bed. Some of the places he thought had electric lights, but he knew that someday electricity would be the norm and kerosene lamps would be a thing of the past. Little Feller came over to him and jumped onto his lap, and of course all the while licking his face. The Preacher thought, *what a wonderful gift the Lord had given him in a small dog that filled in some of his loneliness.* He was startled as he heard a faint knock on the door.

The Preacher asked, "Who is it? What do you want at this time of the night?"

"It is me," replied a male voice.

The Preacher said to him, "I am sorry but you have me mistaken for someone else." The Preacher let him in to his room.

The man smiled and said, "I met you earlier tonight at the high school gymnasium."

The Preacher responded, "I met so many people this night, so forgive me if I do not remember your face or your name."

The young male looked like he was in his early or middle thirties.

The Preacher asked, "What is your name and why do you want to see me at this hour of the night?"

"I have two things to discuss with you, and they will not take much time. One is that I came to tell you that one of the board members is not in favor of hiring another minister. He has wanted the position for a long time. I saw how you carry yourself and radiate the love of Jesus, I knew then that you were truly a man of God. The other concerns Deborah Johnsen. We have dated a few times and I would love to make her my bride. I have known her since we were in grammar school together. Her husband, who was killed in France in the last war, we were very close friends and I truly miss him. I thought you could put in a good word for me after you get to know me better."

The Preacher thought, then he responded, "You have put me in a strange position asking me to bless your relationship with Deborah. I normally am not in the habit of playing Cupid, but if things work out for you and her, I will be more than happy to give you counseling before you come together as man and wife. It all depends on her if she has those feelings for you. This will have to do for yourself; this is my advice to you. Now, young man, if you will excuse me, I need to pray and prepare myself for tomorrow's services." He showed him out the door and locked it after him. He stayed up praying and asking God for guidance and direction as to what further advice he would offer the young man.

The young man's name was Earl Blackman. He thought there was something gentle about this young man and felt sure he would be a fine husband to Deborah, and a father to her two boys. He prayed a special prayer for the

Deacons, especially the head Deacon. He finally went to bed as he looked at the clock that said 2:30 AM. The minute his head hit the pillow, he was asleep. It had been a trying day, but he knew the direction the good Lord wanted him to go: to guide the people in the church and teach them God's ways.

CHAPTER 4

He had set the alarm for 6 AM. He awoke with a startled expression on his face, then realized where he was and why he had set the alarm. He quickly got up, went into the kitchen, and prepared a pot of coffee while the coffee was brewing. He decided to save some time, so he dressed for his first Sunday, ministering the gospel. He thought of the last time he had dressed with his suit of black along with a Preacher's robe. He looked in the mirror to see how he looked when he noticed the robe had some stains on it, so he decided not to wear it until he had it cleaned. He put his shoes on last, then went into the kitchen as he smelled the fragrance of the coffee. There he found in the icebox a couple of old donuts. So, he filled his cup along with the two donuts and sat down with his Bible, then read a few passages of the Scriptures. He had prayed about it and felt that what he would preach and teach his first Sunday to his new congregation. God had spoken to him through that little inner voice on what to present to the congregation for his first sermon.

As he glanced at the clock, which now said 8:20 AM, he was still on his knees praying and asking God the

Holy Spirit to anoint him in a special way. Of the people he had met the night before, most of them were mere babies in Christ. He knew that his work would be difficult but God the Holy Spirit would give him the wisdom to use the Scriptures to enlighten, rather than preach fire and brimstone. Being gentle and correcting error by building them up, not tearing them down. It had been so long that he had felt a great need to uphold and exalt the Lord. Some ministers have a tendency to wound the parishioners, but he had always been one to exhort and comfort God's sheep.

He was startled when he heard the front door being opened. Instinctively, he knew it was Deborah coming to see if he would be on time. He was just finishing his second cup of coffee when she entered and saw him sitting at one of the tables.

"I came to see if you're ready to meet with the Deacon Board, and would be introduced to the congregation."

He answered her, "Deborah, I will not let you down. After all, you were instrumental in getting the Board to ask me to serve this congregation, a task that is ordained by God by using a tryout for a church. This is totally contrary to the teachings of our Lord Jesus Christ. Scripture is very clear about the selection of a minister. It is God who picks those who are gifted to serve the local church. Remember what I said about the book of Ephesians, how Paul the apostle beautifully presents the five-fold apostolic gifts to the church. Apostles, Prophets, Evangelists, Pastors who are able to teach."

"Oh my!" she exclaimed, looking at the clock. "We have less than 10 minutes to meet in the back room of the church with the Deacon board. Forgive me for completely forgetting that the board members usually meet an hour before the beginning of our services. I have my car. It still runs, come on, it is only a couple of blocks from here, but I think they will understand if we are a few minutes late. Let's go."

They made it to the church with a couple of minutes to spare. Deborah went directly to the boardroom with the Preacher right next to her. They walked into the room where the Deacon board were gathering for prayer. They always try to finish by 9:30 AM before the services starts. They took a few minutes to greet one another until they got to the Senior Deacon.

Ever the charming, humble man of God, as he thought of himself, but he always came across as an opportunist. He said to the Preacher, "Have you prepared a sermon for our congregation? I hope that in the future you will let me and the board read it so that we can make sure what you are about to teach or preach meets our standards that complies with our doctrine. Does that sound good to you?"

The Preacher answered in a beautiful manner, "I believe with all my heart that Christ set me apart as a minister of the gospel. I do not know anywhere in the Bible that states I have to get approval from the Deacon board of my sermons. Do you not agree? I will try to always speak God's truth, therefore, I cannot accept your demand. I will be more than happy if you can show me a Scripture that gives you that authority. Based on what you asked me to do, if you cannot accept this, then there is no need for me to bring the good news to you and the congregation."

One of the other members of the board spoke up and said, "Gentlemen, we are not here nor are we chosen for this position as deacons to critique the minister's message. I am shocked that our Senior Deacon feels that way. Perhaps you have placed the rest of us in a dangerous position, especially when it sounds extremely legalistic. Let me remind you of what the role of a Deacon is. It is found in the sixth chapter of the Book of Acts. I rest my case, and gentlemen, it is time for us to close in prayer. Reverend, will you lead us in prayer?"

"It is always an honor. Let us pray."

All the deacons made their way to the front of the church and sat down in the front pews. The Preacher was the last one to sit down in the first seat of the front row. Swede, Deborah's father stepped to the pulpit to open the services.

"Dear ones, today is a very special day, a memorable day since we have a new minister that will be speaking to our congregation this morning. His name is Leonardo Flynn. I have personally spoke at length with this man of God. I believe that little voice that guides my life, the Holy Spirit, sent this gentleman. I pray that all of you who are present this morning will get to know him better. He comes to us from the state of Texas where he ministered in the same church for several years. He is single due to the death of his wife. When we prepare to vote, please do not take into account that he is single. Another issue that needs to be addressed is waving the number of times we normally ask a minister to audition. I do not like the word audition. Christ did not say we should vote for a minister, but those who are sent by Him. We will vote on Pastor Flynn at the end of our services and we will have a potluck to welcome minister Flynn. If you have any questions regarding the appointment of a minister, we need to remember that Jesus selects each minister that he anoints. My personal belief is that we would spend a lifetime trying to fill a position not ordained by God. With that, please save your questions 'til after the services. Will the choir director come forward and lead us in a couple of worship and praise songs? Amen!"

The choir director stood up and went to the piano

and asked the people to stand. "Please turn to page 101 in your hymnals as we sing, 'How Great Thou Art', a favorite of the church. and Amazing Grace."

Then the Preacher went to the pulpit and asked the people to stand as he led them in prayer. He said, "Please remain standing for the reading of the gospel. Our text for today is found in the fourth chapter of the book of Ephesians verses one to six. I hope to finish this two-part series next week, that's if you select me as your church minister. I want to personally thank you for the privilege of sharing the good news with you this morning. My theme will be: *'Unity in the body of Christ.'* If your Bible is turned to Ephesians chapter four, let us proceed." The Preacher opened his Bible, set it on the pulpit and began to quote by memory. (Ephesians 4:1-6 KJV) 'I, therefore, the prisoner of the Lord, beseech you that ye walk worthy of the vocation wherewith ye are called, with all lowliness and meekness, with longsuffering, forbearing one another in love; Endeavoring to keep the unity of the Spirit in the bond of peace. There *is* one body, and one Spirit, even as ye are called in one hope of your calling; One Lord, one faith, one baptism, One God and Father of all, who *is* above all, and through all, and in you all."

When he finished, he went back to the beginning and began to expound on the meaning of the verses and their importance to a believer. He emphasized what the first verse states, *"forbearing one another in love,"* he made it a point that love, God's *love*, is a love that binds wounds. He stopped for a minute and gazed at the audience as he said, "There are some here today that have been wounded and hurt deeply by insensitive people. They forget or have forgotten what true love is. I want you to know that God loves you and as a member of God's body. He will never forsake you." He continued speaking with his gentle soft voice, but rose it to a higher pitch to drive home a point. As he continued speaking on the power of love, some of the parishioners began to weep because the Holy Spirit was ministering to the people using the Preacher's anointing. He stopped and said, "For those of you who feel wounded by insensitive persons, I want you to come to the front of the pulpit, and so you can allow me to pray for you individually."

It took about 45 minutes for the Preacher to pray for each person who came forward. The Deacons came forward and asked to be prayed for as well, showing that God can reach even those who feel that they are above reproach. His sermon lasted about 30 minutes, as the altar call lasted twice as long. Most of the people stayed in the church, but some walked out and gathered in small clusters in front of the church. All of them were still wondering what had happened inside the sanctuary. The service finally came to an end and the people all said their goodbyes. They had completely forgotten to vote. Even the pot luck was forgotten.

The Preacher was tired as he made his way to his room at the Parsonage. He was welcomed by his little companion, Little Feller. He bent down and picked him up and took him outside. He looked like he would burst when he was finished with what he had to do. He decided to eat some leftovers from the pot luck and had taken a few scraps to give to him and didn't take much time eating them. After he finished eating, he went outside and watched the sunset. The Preacher went back into the bed room. Little Feller wanted to play but the Preacher emotionally drained from the amount of people that he had ministered to. He decided to take Little Feller for a walk. After he returned from his walk, the Preacher found an old sock and played tug-of-war with the dog until they were both tired, so the Preacher decided it was time to go to bed. He quickly changed into his nightclothes and crawled into bed.

The preacher was sound asleep when he heard a loud knock on the door. By this time, Feller was barking and running back-and-forth to the door. The Preacher glanced at the clock and noticed that it was 6:30 AM. He wondered who would knock at his door so early in the morning. As he opened the door, there stood a couple of rough looking men. He asked them what they wanted. The Preacher was trying not to lose his temper, because one of them tried to force his way into the room. With all his strength, he overcame the assault.

"Don't come back here or you will feel the wrath of God."

They left in a huff as they raced away in a small truck. The only people he knew in town were those that he had met prior to Sunday and church members. He wondered who these men were, and why they wanted to hurt him. He glanced at the clock and saw that it was almost 7 AM. He made his way into the kitchen and started to brew a pot of coffee while he dressed. When he was finished dressing, he sat down and wrote a few words in a journal he carried with him. Then, he spent an hour in meditation and prayer. As was his custom, he recited a few scriptures. He then gave thanks to God for the work He had done in the hearts of the people yesterday.

He called over to Feller and said, "You must be bursting at the seams, little guy. You must be hungry, so am I. Let's go to the restaurant and see what we can find."

He still had some scraps from yesterday from the potluck. There was a large amount of food left over.

He said to little Feller, "I know you will like them."

He started to open the door into the restaurant when he heard voices and smelled the cooking of smoked ham. As he stepped inside, there was Deborah, her mother and father, and two small boys, whom he assumed were Deborah's sons.

In unison, they all said, "Good morning, Reverend. We hope you slept well. You're just in time for breakfast. Mother Swensen's specialty, Swedish Pancakes. They will be ready in a few minutes."

Mother Swensen filled him a cup of freshly brewed coffee. They were excited about what had happened in the church services. They all ate the pancakes along with eggs and a healthy cut of ham. Deborah said to the boys when they had finished their food to ask the pastor if they could play with Little Feller.

"Of course you can. He loves being around people. He's only been with me a few days. I almost ran over him when I was traveling the day we arrived in Cambria. He needs to run. His breed has the reputation of a lot of energy."

The boys and Feller ran to the back door and went into the woods behind the restaurant.

Deborah asked the Preacher, "Do you mind if I ask you a question?"

"By no means," he said. "What is the question?"

"We were all taken by surprise that you never once looked at your bible. How much of the bible have you memorized?"

He looked at them with his deep blue eyes and said, "Only what I need to at the moment. I can't give you a better answer than this."

The Preacher needed to excuse himself and had to run an errand in town. He started to get up when the boys came running into the restaurant. They were both out of breath as they had difficulty saying why they were excited.

Both of them said, "Little Feller dug up a person. You better come and see."

Deborah jumped up and finally caught up with the Preacher and the boys. The boys led the way into a deep part of the forest and when they got to the spot, they found Feller digging around a shallow grave.

Little Feller stopped when the Preacher said forcefully, "Stop that, Feller."

He leaned down and dug away a large portion of the shallow grave. He asked Deborah to go back and call the police. She also took the twins with her. She was trying to keep the boys from being traumatized by seeing the sight of a dead person. It didn't take long for the Sheriff to arrive with a cadre of law enforcement officers. He introduced himself to the Preacher as Martin Grady.

"I hope you didn't neutralize the crime scene?"

"The digging, you see, was done by my little dog, a Jack Russel Terrier. In fact, he was the one who discovered the body."

At this time the County Coroner arrived and examined all around the site. He finally dug up the remains and said, "This is a brief report. You will get a better report when I do the autopsy. The remains are those of a late teenager. Based on the condition of the deterioration, she has been deceased around two years. I'll have a full report in about a week. I'm having to work long hours because one of my men is home with a broken leg."

They loaded the body on a stretcher and carried the remains to the lot behind the restaurant. The Sheriff said that they were all done and did not speculate as to who, where, and why the girl was killed. He would have more to say as soon as he had the full autopsy.

The Preacher kept thinking who would do such a heinous crime. He knew that what he had seen a few nights ago was the girl. As he continued to think about the girl, God had let her appear to him only. He should have followed up after he saw the aberration. He walked over to the restaurant to make himself a cheese-burger and a soda.

When he got there, there were people eating at a table.

Deborah said, "Come on in; we are fixing an early dinner. Do you like cheese burgers and french fries?"

"You bet I do. I came over to see what I could find in the kitchen, and I found you and your family. I'll stay on one condition; I get a glass of milk or a soda."

"How do you like your meat cooked?"

"However you make them."

"One medium with onions and a plate of fries and soda."

They all sat down at a table as they asked the Preacher to give thanks for the blessing and for the Sheriff and his men to find the killer and bring him to justice. He also prayed for the girl's family.

After they were all finished eating, the Preacher asked a question, "Did they have any unsolved murders or missing girls that had been unresolved?"

Mr. Swensen answered, "Yes, as a matter of fact, two years ago, a young girl named Mary Owens went missing. They arrested a young Mexican boy for her death. It was a swift trial, along with a lot of people upset that they tried him without a body. I felt that he was railroaded on circumstantial evidence. His parents attended church for a while. The board voted 3/2 to shun them. They finally left the church. Based on what the other three deacons did, it is disgusting, supposedly men of God. I stayed in the church because of the members who were appalled that some men are very bigoted racist. My personal feelings about the remains found today was the body of Mary Owens. Manuelo Bustamante was found guilty of her murder, a travesty of justice."

The preacher sat in his chair as tears came to his eyes. In his heart, he knew that bigotry is still rampant in the Lord's Bride. He was interrupted by the adults at the table who asked him if he was alright.

"Yes, I'm fine," he answered. We must protect all of our youth. We are approaching a new year. We should remember that our Lord gave us instructions, on how to raise our children, He said, *'Go ye therefore, and teach all nations, baptizing them in the name of the Father, and of the Son, and of the Holy Ghost' (Matthew 28:19 KJV).* Hedonism has replaced faith; bigotry for love. I'm afraid that we may usher in another world war, in the not-too-distant future. Today, we have a choice: follow Christ's teachings and recommit our lives to Him. Mother Swensen, would you mind getting me a cup of coffee and a slice of your strudel. Perhaps you will join me in singing a few songs. I don't have my guitar, but I understand Deborah plays the piano. There is a nice one in the back room. Let's finish our desert and then we can worship for a while."

They all made their way to the back room, sang and worshiped the Lord for almost an hour.

The Swensen's said, "We must put the boys to bed, perhaps we will see you in the morning. Good night." Before he left, they said, "Why don't you move into the parsonage?"

"Thank you for asking. I took the liberty of moving in last night. I slept like a baby in a very comfortable bed."

The Preacher awoke as the Sun was rising, so he decided it was time to get up. He went into the kitchen and started a pot of coffee while he showered. He thought to himself, *a new concept of bathing for most of the common people.* The church members had installed one in the parsonage bathroom last Friday, and completed the installation Saturday. He finished his bathing and then dressed, along with taking Little Feller for his morning ritual. He had bought some dry dog food for Feller and as soon as he set it on the floor, he rushed to the plate and started eating the food. The Preacher started laughing the way the little dog approached the food. He was cautious until he took his first bite, then it was gone in an instant. He then stooped down and picked him up and hugged him. Of course, he responded by licking the Preacher's face like he was thanking him for giving him dry food. The Preacher also had a bone that he had brought from the pot luck and gave it to him.

The Preacher sat for a few minutes thanking God for sending him to Cambria. He then went into the living room with his second cup of coffee, sat down in the new easy chair, and started reading a few Proverbs. He thought back to yesterday when the body of the girl was uncovered. He said to himself, *I felt the weapon was a knife, and a gun was not used in the crime,* he knew he was right. He felt the sheriff was not an honest person. He had no proof, just a feeling, one of the gifts of the spirit, the distinguishing of spirits. He wondered if the officer was involved with the mobsters who were flooding the USA with illegal alcohol. He thought to himself, *you cannot legislate morality, make it against the law and human nature takes over. They forget the power of the Holy Spirit.*

He decided to get some breakfast, and since it was a nice warm day, he would go to the sea shore and meditate as he walked. He walked into the restaurant and there were a lot of people sitting, drinking coffee, and eating Mother Swensen's strudel. Some of the people were on their way to work, others were a mixture of fishermen, farmers and tourist.

Deborah came over to him and said, "What can I get

you this morning?"

"Two poached eggs, a large piece of strudel, and a cold glass of milk. That's all. I had too much to eat yesterday so I thought I would fast a couple of meals."

She answered, "I don't know where you get the will power to fast and not be tempted."

He said, "It's a gift from God." His breakfast arrived and he ate in haste.

Deborah asked, "Where are you off to today?"

"This morning, after I leave, I am going to the ocean and visit some people who haven't been to church in quite a while. While I'm there, I want to check out the beauty of the Pacific Ocean." He finished his breakfast, excused himself and said, "I will probably see you for dinner. Bye."

CHAPTER 5

The Preacher was strolling along on the beach when he looked out about two miles. He noticed a fishing crawler that sounded like it was having engine problems. The smokestack was billowing out dark smoke and fire. The boat was headed for an inlet where fishermen buy gas and bait for their boats. He decided to see what was about to happen as he started running and telling Little Feller to keep up with him. He had to climb over some rocks to get to the small beach. About the time the boat was headed for shore, it blew up. He stripped his shirt and took his shoes off and dove into the icy water. With powerful strokes, he made it to the boat within a few minutes. When he reached the wreckage, he glanced around and spotted a small dingy made for two which was filling with water and about to sink. He reached the spot where the men were clinging to it.

He asked them, "Who has the most serious injury?"

The older man who responded was the captain. "Art over here is the only one who can swim, but I think he has a dislocated shoulder."

The Preacher said, "The rest of you, hang on to a plank or something that will float." He grabbed the injured fisherman. It took him a few minutes to reach the shore. The tide was coming in which made it difficult for the small fleet of rowboats to make any head way.

The Preacher said, "This man has some major head injuries and a busted shoulder. Wrap him in blankets and call an ambulance." He, then dove into the water for the second time. He swam out and reached another fisherman who could not swim and told him to relax and try not to jump on his back. He made it to shore within a few minutes, dropped the man on the sand, and returned to the wreckage. He saw that the captain was being picked up as he arrived. The last survivor said that a teenager was trapped in the wheel house. The man said he could swim but he had hurt his legs and was unable to move them. The Preacher instructed him to turn over and float as he would stroke for the two of them.

The Preacher returned to the wreckage for the last time just as a large part broke off and sunk. He dove underwater and saw the wheel house. He noticed a young man was breathing in an air trap in a small space. He told the young man to take a deep breath as the Preacher grabbed him by the arm and swam to the to the top. He told the young man to let him do the stroking as he pulled the young man with one arm and stroked with the other. They made it to shore as the last of the wreckage sank to the bottom. The cargo had been bootleg whiskey as a few of the bottles made it to the shore where the tide would continue depositing what was left of them.

People were waiting with hot coffee and a warm blanket. He wrapped it around him as he remembered Little Feller while he called out his name. One of the watchers said that the Johnsen twins had the dog as he pointed to a small shack. He could hear his bark as the boys came over with the dog about the time the Sheriff walked over to where he was sitting, getting his strength.

The Sheriff said, "How's it going, Preacher? I hear you are quite a hero; saved four people, one being rushed to the hospital and the other men are over there by the bonfire. Everyone says they have never seen a stronger swimmer. My question is, did you see the whiskey bottles they were hauling as cargo?"

The Preacher responded, "How could I not when I had to swim through a lot of glass and a handful of unbroken ones. You should ask those behind you if they were able to salvage any."

The Sheriff said, "I already have. I wanted to hear it from you."

The Preacher asked, "Are you accusing me of being a bootlegger?"

"No, just a routine question, Preacher."

The Preacher said, "I understand you have a job to do."

The sheriff asked him if he would write down what he saw and the actions he took. "You are an eye witness. I hope you don't mind."

"No not at all Sheriff. Come around in the afternoon tomorrow since I will be home, if that's okay."

"Great."

"I'll see you tomorrow afternoon."

As he left, the Preacher wondered about the sheriff if he was involved with the bootleggers. The way the people are drinking with the current law, referred to as the law of prohibiting the selling of drinkable alcohol of any sort. He thought, *the tragedy is that the drinking of moonshine in its place does as much damage to the body as bottled whiskey.* It's available at underground casinos and other places which add to the problem. He thought, *how sad that acute alcoholism is also rampant in the United States.* One of the problems in making a certain alcohol called Moonshine is the addiction it causes. You cannot legalize morality. Humanism takes over and the Holy Spirits guidance in some instances is ignored. He was startled, when he heard a familiar sound. It was Little Feller's bark as he was running with two boys – Deborah's twin boys.

The Preacher said, "Boys, are you ready to go home? I don't want your mother to be worried about you, so let's go."

It took a few minutes to walk back to the restaurant. As they approached the restaurant and saw a large crowd gathered in front, he and the boys made their way to the entrance and were shocked at the amount of people who had crowded into such a small building. When he walked in, some of the people came over where he was standing and started shouting in unison.

"God bless the Preacher!"

He said, "Please, don't exalt me. There is only one God – the Father, Son and Holy Spirit."

With this, the crowd responded and said, "We pray for your leadership and ask you for your blessing."

He said, "Amen as to your blessing, but I'm concerned for those who were hurt physically and for the safety of our fishermen and their families." He stopped and asked everyone to bow their heads and asked God for the community of Cambria to be a Godly one.

A reporter spoke up and said, "Sir, what makes you so sure we need your God in our lives?"

"That is a question asked by many. My answer is very simple – we must believe by faith that He created the heavens and earth. We can accept that His love for His creation was why he sent His Son to atone for our sins. Christ became the mediator for reconciliation between God and man. A simple scripture is that man must confess that Christ is Lord and establishes his relationship between the repentant and God. If you ask God into your heart, you are a new creation, all the old things have passed away and you have been born again. For some of you, the road of life is very wide, but those who believe that Christ died for their sins, the road is narrow, but straight. If you are interested, we have a Sunday morning worship service at 10 AM. I take this moment to invite you to our service. Thank you and may God bless you."

When he finished speaking the people started leaving, but some stayed hoping to speak in private with him. There was a strange looking man with a very thick beard that looked like he always needed a shave. He was built very swarthy with powerful shoulders that looked like his coat was far too small. He had long arms and short squatty legs. Most people would not like to have anything to do with him. He was someone when he opened his mouth to speak, it looked like he was sneering at you.

The man came over to the Preacher and said, "May

I take a moment of your time?"

The Preacher answered, "I need to go to my home and take a bath. I still have a lot of sand and salt dried on my skin. I can give you a moment, what is your question? And to whom am I speaking?"

"Anthony Guardino, I work for the Federal Government Drug and Alcohol division. The question I ask concerns you and what you saw this morning while rescuing the men who were injured in the explosion. What I need to know is if they were transporting illegal cargo known as bootleg whiskey. Did you see any undamaged cases that could be salvaged?"

"Mr. Guardino, I was too busy concentrating on helping those men stay alive. I did not have time to look around underwater or on top. I'm sorry; I can't be of any help to you. Again, I must go clean up. Good bye, sir. Oh, one more question, may I see your credentials?"

The man looked like he would explode as he rushed out the door.

The Preacher made his way to the parsonage and went right to the bathroom and took his second shower. He bathed until he ran out of hot water. He thought how dirty he felt in the presence of evil this afternoon. He wondered how a man could sell his soul to the devil. He thought of all the men and women who would not enter the Kingdom of God, as tears flowed from his eyes. He again thanked God for his guidance to this place and said to the Lord that he would do all in his power to bring hope, peace and joy to the people in Cambria. He was about to step out of the shower and dry off when someone knocked on the door. He shouted out that he was getting dressed and said to please come in. He heard a strange voice with a heavy Spanish accent as he said thank you and sat down on the couch.

The Preacher came out all dressed and refreshed as he said hello to a Mexican couple. He answered in Spanish and asked for their names. The man introduced himself and his wife as Manuelo and Angelina Bustamante. After greeting each other, they asked the Preacher where he had learned his Spanish. He answered that he was brought up by his mother who was from Mexico, and an Irish father named Sean Flynn. They were both ecstatic that he spoke their native language.

The Preacher said to them, "Why did you come to see me?"

They told him how they had come here from a border state, Arizona, about twelve years ago and worked on a farm here in the area. They related to him that they needed help in two issues: one, on the incarceration of their son who was charged with murder on circumstantial evidence, and the other subject was they wanted to purchase a piece of land and asked if he would find out if it was a fair price. They had a dream when they came to the United States for the purpose of one day fulfilling their dream – owning their own land. He asked them where the property was located, and if there were any buildings on the property. They were very expressive as they said there was also a small home on the property.

At this point, the Preacher said he would look into both requests – to their son and the property.

He said, "I would like to invite you to church this Sunday if you can make it."

"Forgive me, Pastor. We attended a few times, but when our son was arrested, we were told by the leadership not to attend again, so we are without a church."

"You come this Sunday as my personal guests. I assure you that in God's house all are welcome. I ask your forgiveness for the way some inconsiderate men who are wrong in what it is to be a Christian."

They said to him that they would, on one condition: he would come to their home after church.

He said, "I wouldn't miss Mexican food when its offered. I'm sorry, but I have a meeting that I cannot miss. It will start in an hour so you will have to excuse me."

They said their goodbyes and said they would see him on Sunday.

The Preacher walked over to the café. As he entered, Deborah was busy with another customer.

She waved to him and said, "Are you here to eat, or for the meeting?"

He responded, "Both."

It was almost 6 PM, so he decided to have a bowl of chicken soup and some crackers, with a large glass of milk. She came over and took his order and handed it to the cook and within a couple of minutes, Deborah brought a large bowl of homemade soup. He was just about to finish the last sip of milk, when in walked the head deacon.

He said, "Please finish your dinner. I understand you will be attending our weekly meeting? I wanted to tell you what I will be discussing this evening a sort of an agenda. I will open the meeting after we all pray. The treasurer will give our financial report. I would, I mean we would like to hear if you have a vision for our church."

The Preacher responded, "I am the pastor and head elder. I will share God's vision for this church. It is God's church and he has placed me as overseer for now. I will elaborate more during the meeting."

The Preacher got up and went to the back room as

the deacon followed behind. The Preacher went directly to the head of the table and sat down. The head deacon looked a little surprised and was slightly agitated. He was not accustomed to taking orders. He decided to go along with what the man of God had to say.

The rest of the board members filled in all together and took their regular seats.

The Preacher spoke up, "I would like to open the meeting with a prayer, then share what God has for this church. He said I will read from the sixth chapter of the Book of Acts. This chapter initiates the duties of a deacon. He or she should be an individual that is willing to serve in any capacity in the local church."

He continued sharing what the scriptures state about leadership in the local church. He made it a point of being a servant first – when Jesus washed the disciples' feet. The Preacher stopped to see the expression and reaction of the men. He paused and focused on each man's eyes. All of them, with the exception of the head deacon, had tears in their eyes. He was clinching his teeth. The Preacher continued and quoted the 4th chapter of the of the Book of Ephesians.

He said, "I have read you the structure of the leadership in the church, Apostles, Prophets, Evangelist, Pastor and Teacher. I don't see the role of the Deacon in the scriptures, other than what is written in the Book of Acts. There is one more passage of scripture that I believe it applies to us all. (Romans 12:3-6 KJV). 'For I say, through the grace given unto me, to every man that is among you, not to think *of himself* more highly than he ought to think; but to think soberly, according as God hath dealt to every man the measure of faith. For as we have many members in one body, and all members have not the same office: So we, *being* many, are one body in Christ, and every one members one of another.' This is God's vision for our church, to return the church as He left it with Christians, placing others first and making disciples of the nations. We have become far too self-serving in our leadership positions. It is very clear that the church has allowed the clergy to become more interested in self-gratification rather than teaching them the true concept of unity. It begins servant first. All we have to do is look at all the different denominations that treat their pastors like they walk on water. Some demand that they be called *Reverend.* In the eyes of God, there are no favorites; we are all equal. If we demand respect, we have not earned the title. I ask this question to all; does God rule your heart, or do you think you're above reproach. I knew a man once who lived off of others. He claimed he had a special dispensation from God. God said that He would supply all of our needs, that includes a job. The disciples left everything to serve, but they were chosen for a special call as the Apostles. The Holy Spirit gives us instructions. We must put our faith in Him. Pray about your current role as a Christian and where you stand with Him. I will be open for discussion individually. Just contact me by next Sunday. I look forward to meeting with each one of you individually. I will be gone for the next couple of days on some urgent business. Good night. It was my pleasure to be here with you and for you to hear my heart."

The Preacher left the meeting and went home to the parsonage. He was planning on going to San Quentin Prison and the office of drug and alcohol in Paso Robles. As he walked to his home, he felt an uneasy feeling. He recognized that evil presence. He laughed within himself thinking that if only the evil presence knew what awaited him. God knew what was about to happen; God had to give the devil permission to physically harm him. He reached the parsonage and was about to open the door when all went black.

CHAPTER 6

He woke up as he felt a wet tongue on his face and realized it was Little Feller licking his face, but sitting in the corner chair was an unfamiliar face.

The man said, "Are you finally awake, Mr. Preacher? I came to your home and saw that the front door was wide open. I came in and saw you lying on the floor with your little dog licking your face as you were coming to. He sure is a cute little guy. My name is Gilbert Snowden. I'm a private investigator for the Federal Government. Here are my credentials, if you don't mind me asking you a few questions."

"Not at all, Mr. Snowden. May I ask why you are here, and what or whom are you looking for?"

"My first question has to do with bootleggers. A man was here asking questions of you two days ago concerning illegal alcohol. We know who he is; a seedy character that is a member of an Eastern mob. He is highly dangerous and always carries a stiletto knife along with a snub-nosed 38. He has served at least two terms in maximum prisons serving eight years total. He was released early both times. He was released a couple of years ago. We know he was involved in two unsolved homicides of women. I need to know what he asked of you and when did he approach you."

"He came to the restaurant yesterday. He specifically wanted to know if I had seen any unopened bottles in the wreckage of the small tugboat that blew up. He passed himself off as a drug and alcohol agent. I knew he wasn't when I asked to see his credentials. His response was very poor. He said he had left it in the hotel. He got a little agitated when I pressed him as for information, but then I left because I had a board meeting of the church. I told him that I couldn't comment on such information. He left in a hurry. That's all I know about him."

The Federal officer said to the Preacher, "This is a private question concerning Deborah Swensen. She was married to a young man who fought in the Great War. I was asked by another agent to ask her a few questions regarding his status as missing in action. Do you think she would be open to a few questions?"

"I believe she would. Based on the law stating, he is finally listed as deceased by our government. Well, as long as it doesn't get her expectations up. Can you insure me thatwhat you ask her is okay?"

"I can assure you that I will be very gentle. In fact, I would hope that you will sit in on the interview. Is this agreeable with you?"

"Yes, I welcome the invitation. Do you have a specific time?"

The Preacher said, "I will arrange for you to meet with her. Call me at the café early in the morning."

"Good, I will call you in the morning. Hope to see you sometime tomorrow."

The Preacher looked at the clock and saw how late it was, yet he needed to shower and change clothes. He also needed to take Feller for his evening constitutional before his bladder burst. They went outside to a chilly night. As they walked along, he noticed that the moon was full as the cloud's passed over, covering and then uncovering the brilliance of its splendor. The uncovering was like a multi colored blanket.

As he was walking back to the Parsonage, he saw a flash of light coming from the forest. He stopped and listened as he heard the sound of a vehicle. He thought in his mind that it sounded like a truck struggling to free its self from a bog. You could also hear the gears being changed, until the roar of the engine sounded like it had been freed. He thought he should quietly go and see what was happening. As he and Little Feller made their way to the wooded area. Little Feller growled very softly, like he sensed he needed to be quiet as they slowly approached the area where the Preacher thought the spot would be. Suddenly, he saw there was a truck being loaded with cases of bootleg whiskey. He dropped to the ground as he pulled Little Feller down with him. They were covered by a large full leaf bush. The Preacher crouched behind the bush that seemed like hours to him. It was close to an hour when he heard voices.

"Let's wrap it up, guys. We have a couple more stops to make to our warehouse, then we take the whole load."

It took them a couple of more minutes, then they left as the truck struggled to get up speed to get to the main road. The Preacher recognized a voice that sent a chill down his back – it was a member of the church.

He stood up and was glad he had brought a flashlight with him. He cautiously walked over to a small shack and thanked the Lord the bootleggers had all left. He looked over the front of the shack and saw a sign that said, *Equipment for Federal Forest Lands*. He looked at the door and saw a large lock on it. He walked up to the door and pulled on the lock as it opened. He went inside and noticed a large locker with large metal doors. This also was closed with a combination lock. He thought to himself if he had to guess it was a locker for weapons and gun powder. He knew the smell of cordite, a chemical compound that is used in the making of gunpowder and dynamite. He was startled as he thought he heard a vehicle coming up the dirt road. The sound was not the same as the truck. He grabbed Little

Feller and closed the door placing the lock in its place. He went behind the same bush as he hid from the bootleggers. He thought to himself he needed his watch, but for some reason, he had not had it repaired. He was concerned about the time. He thought it was around 1:00 or 1:30 AM. He heard two voices coming up a trail. One was the voice of a female and the other a young male.

The young man said to the girl, "Don't act like the last time we were here. I promised to marry you and still you act so cold."

At this point the Preacher stood up and said, "Do you know what you are doing? You are violating one of the most holy commandments: 'thou shall not commit adultery' (Mathew 5:27KJV). I recognize you both. I met you in church this past Sunday. I expect to see you at my house at 11:00 AM and I won't take no for an answer. I was taking my dog for a walk and I had to chase him in here. Both of you go home, and if I hear otherwise, I will call God's wrath upon you."

They ran back to their car as the Preacher heard the car take off at a high speed.

The Preacher had to carry Little Feller back to the parsonage. When they got back to the house, he checked the entire home and made sure that all the windows were closed. One exception was the bedroom. The Preacher liked to have fresh air flowing into the room when he slept. He decided to skip his shower until the morning. It had been a long day and very tiring. He soon fell asleep and dreamed of being in Heaven.

He awoke when he was startled by a sharp shaking of his home. He realized that it was an earthquake. This was a new experience for him. He had heard of quakes and most likely he would experience the feeling again. Soon, he heard dogs barking and howling in the background. He got up and put the coffee on and took Little Feller outside for his morning constitution. He wondered how large a bladder the dog had. They walked back into the house as he feed the little guy his food, then he went into the shower until he almost ran out of hot water. He had to shave with lukewarm water. When finished, he went into the small kitchen next to the dining room. He sat down and had a long prayer in his worship to the Lord. He looked at the clock and went to the restaurant. He needed to eat something that he enjoyed – a slab of Ham and three eggs over medium, and a hot roll or toast, buttered.

The Preacher walked over to the diner and sat down in one of the booths.

Deborah came over and sat down and said, "What did you think of the quake we had this morning?"

He replied, "I don't know what to think. It's the first

time I have experienced the feeling of helplessness, but I understand there are places in the world that experience earthquakes almost daily."

She said, "What are you having for breakfast this morning?"

"Ham and three eggs, and a biscuit… and might as well add a side of fried potatoes," he answered.

"Got it."

Deborah walked over to the kitchen counter and gave the order to the cook. She came back with a cup of coffee and poured one for herself.

"How are things going this morning?" he asked.

"As hectic as always, and as you can see the place is almost full with a late crowd. I think it is due to the quake. People always expect another. That's what they call aftershocks. Here comes one now."

They felt a small rumble and a small shaking.

He said, "I suppose you get used to them. I have a question to ask you if you have time."

"For you I will make the time. What's on your mind?"

"I need to find out who owns that section of land as you approach town. I see the for-sale sign and at the bottom, it states: *small home included.* Do you know who owns it and how much are they asking for it?"

"That's an easy question. My father owns the property and is willing to carry the note at a below the current market rate. The little house is the home I was born in and my brother as well. Who wants to purchase the land?"

"The Bustamante's will be in church this Sunday, and I will get your dad and the couple together so they can discuss terms."

"Sounds good to me," she said.

"Another issue that concerns me is about the area where the girl's body was found. Is it a place where lovers go?"

"I guess so; why do you ask?"

"Before I went to bed as usual, I was walking Little Feller. Last night was no exception. I heard a car coming up the dirt road. A couple of kids were up to what a lot of kids try to do. I scared the heck out of them. They are coming to see me at the parsonage at 11 this morning. I am also expecting a call from a federal officer. He wants to meet with you and I. He will call here to confirm a meeting with you early this afternoon. Just tell him it's okay for us, if it's all right to get together around 2 PM. I hope it's ok with you."

"Reverend, I trust your judgment. I will tell him it's okay for us to meet with him."

"It's 10 AM right now, so I had better finish my breakfast. I have a feeling the two kids will be early. Where are your boys? I haven't seen them since yesterday."

She answered, "My dad had them pulling weeds and raking leaves. They love him dearly, but they have chores that they are expected to do."

"Ask them if they want to babysit Little Feller this afternoon, they can. I will be meeting with the Federal Agent and you. Thanks for a great breakfast. See you later." He walked out and headed for the parsonage.

When he got to the parsonage, the couple was waiting for the Him. His great discernment of people was a gift from God. He ushered them into the house and asked them to sit down on the sofa.

"Before we continue, we will have a few minutes of prayer."

They all knelt down as the Preacher began.

When they had finished the Preacher said, "I want to thank you both for being punctual. I pray that you will receive my counsel. I also pray for both of you that from this day forward, you will start doing God's will and that the actions you are starting today will last a life time for both of you. 'Lord may your blessings be upon this young man and young lady. If it's God's plan for your lives, someday, you will be joined in matrimony. Father I ask for your blessing to be included in Jim and Alice's lives from this day forward. Amen!' I take my prayer life seriously. I will add your names to the list. Now, what are your sur names?"

Jim answered for them both. "My full name is Jim Bradshaw and she's Alice Rivers. I am 18 years old and Alice is 16 years old. Both of us were born here in Cambria. My Father was killed in Europe during the Great War. Mom had to raise me and my younger sister. Alice can tell you her story."

Alice responded, "I was raised by my grandparents on one of the farms. My parents were both killed in a car accident when I was six years old. As far as I know, I am an only child."

The Preacher said, "Both of you have had trauma in your early years which has tainted your concept of Love and Marriage. Marriage is the most sacred commitment a person will experience. Adultery is one of the worst sins, because it is a sin of lust. Let me explain, but first ask me any questions pertaining to our discussion, but wait until I finish. When God created Adam and Eve, they were sinless as He joined them together through the act of marriage. He pronounced them as husband and wife. He also said the two shall become one. They were expected to subdue and rule the earth, and procreate. This is the standard for all marriages, to be joined together by God. This is the covenant of marriage. Living together out of wedlock violates the concept of a virgin marriage. Society blames the woman more than the man when they come together before marriage. The man loses his virginity as well."

At this point, the Preacher stopped and said, "Are there any question? If not, I have a few statements that may shed light on how much Bible Knowledge you have. First, do you understand the term *Born Again*?"

They both looked at him as if to say, *this man doesn't know what he is talking about.*

"One more question, do you know who Christ said He was?"

They both answered, "No, sir."

At this point, the Preacher asked another question of both of them. "How would you both like to be in full time ministry?"

Jim said, "My grandfather was a minister, but he died shortly after I was born. Mom used to tell me of some of the revivals he held. She said that people would come from all over to hear his sermons. She said that people would get healed when, ah... what did she call it?... yes,

I remember now. *Come forward and receive Jesus.* What does that mean, sir?"

The Preacher responded, "When people are touched by God through a sermon, they go forward and ask Christ for forgiveness. This is called an 'Act of faith.'

Jim said, "Ever since I was little, I have felt that something or someone was calling me."

The Preacher answered, "Most likely, it is the Holy Spirit calling to you. Do you hear a voice as well?"

"Yes, sir; at times I do, but mostly in my head. Why do you ask me about hearing a voice? I'm not dreaming, am I?"

"No, you are not. God has many ways of communicating with us. Others see visions, some see God in their dreams, and most of us, God speaks to us through the Scriptures. My question still stands, would you like to go into full time ministry? It is a lonely road to travel, but you will never look back if God has touched you."

Alice said, "What about me? I think it would be very exciting to see people who are hurting change their lives because of Christ."

The Preacher said, "I notice that it is getting late and I have another person I have to meet at the restaurant. I want to ask you to pray, a closing prayer with me. Is that all right with you both?" The two nodded in unison. "Good. Let us kneel here in the parsonage. Repeat after me: Dear Jesus, I ask for forgiveness of all the wrongs I have committed in my life. I want to be a child of God. I am sorry for my past life. I dedicate my life to serve you. I don't understand so many things about you, but I am willing to learn from you. From this day forward, I promise."

At this moment they both broke into tears and were sobbing. Both were shedding tears of repentance. The Preacher reached over and hugged them both. He assured them that what they had done would become more real each day. He asked them if they each had a Bible. They said yes, and that their family has one. "Good," he said. "I want you to both read the Gospel of John. To make notes and meet with me once a week in the evening. One more thing, do not violate the sacred vow of marriage and come together. You must abstain from body contact until you are ready for marriage. I would be honored to perform the ritual. Well, we will talk some more."

As they left and ran to their car, the Preacher went to the restaurant smiling all the way and praising the Father for leading the young couple to him. He walked into the restaurant still smiling as he saw Deborah waiting on a customer.

CHAPTER 7

Deborah came over and sat at the same table with the Preacher. She was smiling as she outwardly seemed happy.

The first thing she said, "An agent from the Federal Government called and said he was on his way. He would be here around 1 PM. It's now 12:30, so he should be here soon. I need to ask you a personal question. Do you know what he wants?"

"He wants some personal information concerning your husband."

"Do you think I should speak with him? He said he discussed it with you and I said only if you could sit in on the conversation, would you mind?"

The Preacher said, "Of course not. I feel it is an honor. Did he set up a time for you to meet?"

"I told him a good time would be between one and two. Do you want to order lunch or wait on him?"

"Let's wait on him. Besides, I notice the special of the day is a BLT sandwich, French fries, and a beverage."

"Okay," she said.

The Fed arrived and glanced around the room to see who was there. He went over where the Preacher was sitting with Deborah. They all exchanged pleasantries, along with all the laughing at the same time. It was nice to see an agent of the government with a good sense of humor.

Agent Snowden said to Deborah that it was a pleasure to finally meet her. He explained that he was here on a dual investigation. They were short of agents at this time. Early retirement had taken its toll on the number of agents available.

The Preacher asked the first question. "Have you had any break as to who the individual or individuals who are responsible for the Tug Boat blowing up?"

"As of this date, we don't have a corroborating witness. You are the only one that has related an accurate account. The captain won't answer our questions so we are stymied as to how it happened."

"One thing that hinders us is irresponsible citizens fail to come forth and report what they witness."

The Preacher responded, "When I hear that people fail to live up to their responsibilities, I think of what our Savior had to endure in His mock trial. The Pharisees solicited false witnesses and brought charges against Him. Pilate strongly opposed the charges, but he was afraid of the

Emperor blaming him for the trumped-up charges would reach Rome and cast a cloud upon him."

All the while, Deborah is listening to their conversation. She said, "We are directed by the scriptures to tell the truth, so many souls don't want to get involved in political issues."

The Preacher said, "That we would know the truth, and the truth would set us free. One of the reasons the Pharisees are held guilty of killing our Lord is that they lied about Christ, thus they are guilty for all eternity."

The agent said, "It's getting very theological around here. I'm hungry and would like your special. How about you, Reverend? Do you want the special also?"

"I am hungry, Deborah. I'll have the same."

When she went into the kitchen, the Preacher asked the Agent if he had any news concerning Deborah's deceased husband.

"Yes, I did. I had gotten in touch with the Military Adjutant General's Office. I was told that there were few men in a French Military Hospital, and that there were three or four men that fit the description." He continued, "Preacher, let's finish our lunch, then resume our conversation."

Deborah brought her lunch with a plain cheese on rye bread. They sat and talked about the major problem of people drinking when the law said it is prohibited.

The Preacher said to the Agent, "What do you think about alcohol? Does the Bible also prohibit the use of alcohol?"

He laughed and said, "I thought you didn't want to hear about theological topics? Well, no; it does not prohibit alcohol. Paul the Apostle when writing a letter to Timothy recommends that he drink a little wine for his stomach. Based on the water of those days, some could be bitter due to an excess of alkali. The wine would take some of the bitterness that caused him stomach problems. The custom of those days was to serve wine with their meals. The Roman soldiers drank water with wine because of the bitterness of the water. Our Lord was offered this on the cross, yet he denied it. The Old Testament in Proverbs cautions the people of drinking alcohol to excess, as to getting drunk. As far as I know, there is no scripture that prohibits alcohol. Noah made wine and became inebriated and shamed himself. I hope this answers your question. My feeling is this, if you have a parishioner who struggles with alcoholism, a minister should abstain from wine or other types such as vodka, gin and other well-known alcoholic beverages; beer is the most widely used."

At this point Deborah said, "Can we change the subject, Mr. Snowden?"

The Preacher interrupted, "We are not any closer to solving the murder of the girl found dead, while a young man sits in prison for a crime he didn't commit. New evidence was found that would clear Manuelo Bustamante. The body of the girl was exhumed and it was found that she had been stabbed to death. The coroner did not perform an autopsy when he should have. He is under investigation as we speak. I think he should be fired and arrested for being complacent."

Deborah said, "Why haven't the Sheriff and the DA reopened the case, and let an innocent young man rot in a cell for almost two years. His lawyer gave a lousy defense as I see it. They listened to the bigot's that screamed for blood. His parents used to attend our church but an insensitive head Deacon asked them not to come back. Can you help speed the process up, Agent Snowden?"

"I can't promise to get him out, but I will look into what's holding up the new trial."

The Preacher said, "I will call the State DA and get more information, if he can push them harder. I will ask our church people to do two thigs: one – pray daily for his release, and then sign a petition for the injustice done to him. I will make it my priority to pray to the Lord daily on his behalf. Let us pray for guidance."

After he said a prayer for unity and love, he asked

Deborah if they could move to the back room where they would have more privacy. She agreed and told the waitress not to disturb them unless an emergency arises. They got up and sat at one of the tables in the back room.

Agent Snowden said, "I recently came across a letter sent to all federal agencies concerning a patient that had been hospitalized since 1919, almost ten years. It said that a man about thirty years of age had walked away from a veteran's mental unit. He is not dangerous, but has been diagnosed as having amnesia, but recently, he started having dreams of an area he felt that he had lived in. It turns out that he was dreaming of a community similar to Cambria. I made a couple of calls and recently found out that he fit the description of the missing in action Soldier. If he is the man from this area, it could be your husband. He joined the Army in 1917, he also had a wife and a set of twin boys, born after he came home on furlough. He started remembering his dreams in full detail. Those who have had amnesia for years, I was told it was a good sign, but in some cases, the memory does not return completely, small portion or a complete recovery. He had been captured by German soldiers near the end of the war, and of course, he didn't know who he was. He had no papers or any ID of any kind. He was liberated at the end of the war. They found him wandering the streets in France and was hospitalized in a veteran's hospital in France. He was then sent to an Army hospital where he has been for about eight years. One day, they checked his room and he was gone. He took a bus from the hospital in Maryland to Pennsylvania, and from there we don't know. He had money saved for being a prisoner of war and asked for some of his pay. We think he may have caught a train heading West, but to where, we don't know. I believe he will show up here. The Federal Government doctors asked me to contact them if he shows up. They want to know if he has regained his full memory or even just partial. There is a veteran's hospital in San Francisco. The Doctors advice that you should be as loving and caring, but don't rush him in thinking he is one hundred percent cured. He has been a very sick man that needs a lot of love and understanding. Ten years have changed you, but in his mind, he lives in the year 1919. You, your parents, and his sons will be strangers to him. If he shows up, welcome him, but convince him to continue seeking psychiatric care offered by the Veterans Administration. He has earned it."

Deborah sat in silence listening to Agent Snowden. She wanted to respond, but she was taking her time. She finally broke. She could not hold it back as she started sobbing as tears flowed from the depth of her soul. She was finally able to speak, as her sobbing stopped.

She finally said, "From the time I received a telegram saying my husband was missing in action, I have been hoping each day that today would bring news that he was alive. I prayed to God for him each day until a couple of years ago. I had resolved myself that he was dead. Now, you bring news that this man may be my husband? The pain I felt and the loneliness that I have had to live with… now, I'm not even sure that I still love him."

At this juncture, the Preacher, in his gentle manner, spoke with clarity and authoritative as he said, "Deborah, mental illness is very difficult to deal with. People who suffer amnesia requires that the family be very understanding and need God's strength to bring comfort to all the members of his immediate family. It takes a wise individual to provide Godly wisdom and compassion. The wife shouldn't think that she has to be the pillar of strength. We should wait and see first if it is your husband, then call them altogether and ask for their input as to how to pursue the issue of accepting him back, as a family member. Doesn't this make sense to you? I believe that God has allowed you to suffer because you will be the one who will restore your love. We sometimes think it is unfair. Scripture states that He won't allow us to take on more than we can handle."

Deborah and the Federal Agent sat their dumfounded at his wisdom and counsel. They both agreed and said that it was the right solution in approaching the situation. The clock struck 4:30 PM. Deborah excused herself and left to go home to share the news with her parents.

The Preacher said to the Agent, "What is your first name?"

"Like you, Reverend; it's a Hispanic name from my father's side – Gilbert, but everybody calls me Gil."

"Gil, I sensed that you were holding something back about her ex-husband. Do you mind telling me what it is?"

"Preacher, I did not tell her that one side of his face is scarred and disfigured from being burned and gassed in Germany. I am told that he is very self-conscience and ashamed of what he looks like."

"As Deborah's minister, she needs to be told. By not telling her, it will be almost impossible to bring a healthy reconciliation. I will tell her this evening."

Gil said he had to leave. He stated he had a solid lead on some Bootleggers, further up the coast, close to San Siemian. As he left, the Preacher felt that his heart would burst on what he heard from agent Snowden and the pain he witnessed and heard from Deborah. He got up to leave when Deborah came into the room and asked the Preacher if Agent Snowden had held back something. He looked at her with only a person of God can do.

"Yes, please sit down." He told her and was surprised that she calmly accepted her answer. He asked if he could pray with her.

"Of course," she answered.

He prayed a prayer of strength and that compassion would be the love that would prevail. The Preacher left and went home to prepare for the mid-week service. Deborah sat there weeping softly… praying and thanking God to lift this burden from her heart and replace it with the love she had for her husband when they first got married. The words ringing in her ears, *'for better or worse till death do us part'* as she got up and went back to work.

CHAPTER 8

It was early Thursday morning when the Preacher awoke from a sound sleep. He slowly made his way to the bathroom and decided to take a shower; but before he got into the shower, he took Little Feller out for his morning routine.

After they came back into the house, he started a pot of coffee to perk while he showered and shaved. He reflected on last night's church gathering. He shared his vision for the church and asking his parishioners to come forward for prayer, to ask God the Holy Spirit to guide each as to their spiritual gift. He taught out of the book of 1Corinthians 12, and how important it is for the Body of Christ to grow spiritually. He thought, *how quick most of the people in attendance responded when he asked each one to state what they thought was their gift in the body of Christ.* He was pleased with the attitude of the church body. He said he would continue next Wednesday.

He went into the kitchen and poured himself a cup of coffee. As he sat at the table, in deep meditation and prayer, he heard that inner voice – a clear message from the Lord as to his approach to the church members. Clearly, the Lord said, *"I am pleased in your love for the souls I have placed in your care. Love them deeply and they will respond in return."* He shed a few tears as he was travailing in his spirt. He needed encouragement from the Lord.

He finished his morning devotionals and glanced at the clock and saw what time it was: 8 AM. He had checked the bus schedules from Cambria to Paseo Robles. He had a two-hour wait before he had to leave. He had time to eat breakfast and ask Deborah if she would allow her boys to babysit Little Feller. He grabbed his overnight bag with his toiletries and a change of clothes. He picked up Little Feller and made his way to the restaurant.

CHAPTER 9

As the Preacher walked into the Café, he noticed that there was a large group of people gathered around on one of the tables. He knew intuitively that Deborah's husband had made it to Cambria, and some of the people who knew him were welcoming him and asking all types of questions, such as where had he been all these years, had he been in a coma, or were his wounds taking so long to heal. Deborah spotted the Preacher as he sat at the counter when the waitress took his order. He did not want to interrupt the reunion between Deborah and her husband Kyle. The twins were sitting next to their father looking at his scarred face. Both spotted Little Feller on the floor next to the Preacher, so they rushed to ask the Preacher if they could play with him.

The Preacher answered, "Ask your mother if it's okay, and now that your father has come home, you should get to know him; you should love him."

They both asked, "How do we love him?"

"Ask God how to love him. He will show you how much He loves us."

Deborah glanced over to where the Preacher was sitting and smiled at him. She motioned for him to come to their table. He got up to move, but had to pass the small crowd that had circled Kyle. As he approached the table, the small crowd made way for him to sit down.

He said, "It is my pleasure to meet you. May I call you Kyle? I've heard so much about you from your wife. She is a rare type of woman. She is what I call a true woman of God. She shows it by her kind and considerate actions, and by how she treats others. When I first came to Cambria, she treated me with Christian love. I'm honored to be her Pastor."

Kyle looked at him and said, "Thank you for your kind words about my wife. As you know, we were just kids when we first married, and then I went into the Army, so I never thought that I would not see her for almost ten years. I remember when I was taken captive by the Germans, then one day, there was a bombing barrage and that's all I remember. Until about a month ago, I started getting flashbacks of my life here in Cambria and finally, it all came back to me. So, here I am."

The Preacher said, "Kyle I have to catch a bus to Paso Robles. I may be gone until Friday, but I hope to finish my business by tonight. We will get together when I return. Perhaps, this Saturday? Oh, I almost forgot, can the boys take care of Little Feller while I'm gone?"

"No problem, Preacher; it's our pleasure."

"Thank you."

It took five minutes for the Preacher to walk to the Bus Terminal. He looked at the clock in the waiting room, and saw that he had about ten minutes before it arrived. He sat down and prayed to himself, thanking God for the reunion between Kyle and Deborah. He knew that it would take some time for them both to adjust to one another. He reflected on the two weeks he had been here in Cambria, and what God had accomplished in such a short time. He trusted in God for everything as the Holy Spirit wanted him to accomplish. He was committed to initiate each phase of Biblical life. The people in the church had been without a shepherd far too long. They were like sheep without a shepherd and downcast. Sheep have a natural flaw, that when they lay down and roll onto their back, they are unable to right themselves. He thought about the word downcast that describes this characteristic – the solution: workers are needed to teach people the morals and values of God.

He knew that his time in Cambria would not be a long stay, yet he would stay as long as the Lord wanted him to. The Holy Spirit gave him new orders. He was startled as the bus pulled into the terminal, as the loud speaker announcing the arrival of the ten thirty morning bus. He boarded the bus and found a seat close to the driver and noticed his name tag said Jake Hawkins.

"How are you this morning, Jake?"

Jake responded, "This back is killing me. I picked up a piece of shrapnel in France during the Great War. I was an ambulance driver, and a mortar shell hit the ambulance, flipped me and the ambulance. In the process, a small piece of the mortar shrapnel is still in my back. The doctors said that one day in the future, it would either surface or make me an invalid." He abruptly stopped and realized, "Why am I saying all this to you? Are you a psychic?"

"No. It so happens that I'm a minister and believe that the Lord Jesus Christ can heal you. All you have to do is let me pray for you and believe in your heart that He can, and that He will."

"I don't know about this hocus pocus praying for healing. I believe in God, but I doubt that He can."

"I promise that by the time we get to Paso Robles, you will be healed and the shrapnel will be gone."

"If I let you pray for me, where will you do it?"

"Right where you sit and I will take care of the people." The Preacher stood up and told them what he was going to do, and asked them if it was alright for him to pray for Jake before they took off for Paso Robles.

Most of them agreed. But some said, "We know your kind of healing. It's bogus."

A man stood up and said, "Don't you recognize who he is? He's the minister that saved those four men from drowning last week. It was in all the papers. Go ahead. It's okay with us."

Jake turned off the engine and said, "Go ahead."

The Preacher put his hands on the spot where the wound was and said a simple prayer in the name of Jesus Christ. Everyone on board heard and saw the miracle. There was a loud noise as if a tree branch had been broken.

Jake sat in his seat for a few minutes and wept tears of joy. "I believe! I believe! Thank you, Lord, for having mercy on me."

The rest of the people sat in a daze at what had happened in their presence. As always, there were skeptics along with a few believers, but the fact was for those who were Christians, it strengthened their faith. Jake finally started the bus and took off for Paso Robles.

It took almost two hours to reach their destination. As the people got off, a few of them came over to the Preacher and asked what time the services were held on Sunday. They were all from the Cambria area and so was Jake. He cornered the Preacher and thanked him for healing him.

The Preacher answered, "It was Jesus who healed you. I am only obeying what God had spoken to me – to board the bus, and lay hands on the bus driver for healing."

Jake asked the Preacher if he would join him for lunch at the café. He said that Dodie, the lady who ran the café was a staunch Christian woman. They found a seat at an empty table. Dodie a large woman with a radiant smile that made her face radiate. She came over to the table.

"Jake what are you doing in Paso Robles on such a fine day?"

"Dodie, I'm on a special run. One of the men had an emergency, so I volunteered."

Dodie asked Jake why he looked so at peace with himself. She asked him if anything had changed, so Jake proceeded to tell her what the Preacher had done prior to them leaving Cambria.

Dodie said to the Preacher, "Are you an angel?"

"The Preacher burst out laughing and kept trying to compose himself as he stated, "Where did you get such an idea? Can you see any wings coming out of my back?"

She kept persisting on staying on the subject of angels. She continued, "Doesn't it say somewhere in the

Bible that we would entertain them?"

"I believe so, but it escapes me right now the chapter and verse. They are sent from God in time of great need like special assignments. The Book of Acts is a good reference when Peter was in prison. God sent an angel to release his chains. God works in ways that we don't always understand."

Jake said, "Dodie, I need to order lunch for the both of us. I have to be in Santa Maria, and then turn around and back to Paso Robles by 5 PM. I want a cheeseburger and fries, and a large glass of tea. How about you, sir? Go ahead and pick anything from the menu, or you can order the same thing as mine."

"The cheeseburger sounds good. I'll take the same except the tea. Give me a large glass of milk."

Dodie said, "Great."

In a few minutes, Dodie came back with both plates. They prayed for the food as they were not disappointed. They smacked their lips on the delicious tasting cheeseburgers. Jake finished first and looked at his wristwatch. He jumped up as he swallowed the last morsel. He put a five-dollar bill on the counter.

He said to the Preacher, "See you on the way back, if you're still here. I should be back by 6 PM. Dodie I hope that covers the bill." Then he walked over to the waiting bus.

As he closed the door, it can be heard in the speaker, "All aboard! Next stop Santa Maria."

Dodie came over to the Preacher and asked if there was anything more that she could do for him.

"Yes, I need to know two things. One, where is the drug and alcohol office, and number two, where is the newspaper office?"

"They are fairly close to each other. Two blocks from here and you will see the County Court house, and then around the corner from there is the newspaper office."

"Dodie, let me set your mind at ease. The tests that you had for cancer are negative. The only thing is they will recommend you to go on a strict diet. Thanks again for your wonderful food and all your help… and oh, keep watching for angels. You never know when you will encounter one." As he walked out the door, he smiled at her.

Standing at the stairs of the courthouse was a tall muscular man with premature white hair. He carried himself with a look of assurance. He stopped and greeted the Preacher with an assurance and good demeanor for a government employee.

As the Preacher approached the man, he said to him,

"Sir, can you tell me where the Drug and Alcohol office is?"

As he smiled, a smile that was infectious, he said, "I'm your man. Come into my office." He walked over to a small hole in the wall with a door, and barely enough room for a desk and two chairs. The office also had a couple of phones, plus a file cabinet and a picture of the current President of the United States. He finally came and sat down at his desk and said, "What can I do for you?"

The Preacher said, "First, my name is Leonardo Flynn, the minister of the Cambria Local Christian Church. As to why I am here, that is to check with you about an agent and a thug who tried to pass himself off as a Drug and Alcohol Agent. Needless to say, he gave himself away when I asked him for his ID card, but of course, he was unable to produce one."

At this point Agent Ryan Smith said, "Did this fellow resemble a Gorilla when he walked from the waist down? His suit was too tight, as if he would tear the arms from the seam? Did he have a full head of hair, but his hair line extends almost to his eye brows? Also, is he very dark complexed and has a very heavy Sicilian accent? Well, he is a sadistic killer and likes to kill with a stiletto, a special knife, and loves to use a snub-nosed 38 special. If he comes around again, contact the State Police. He has been a suspect of mine on some killings in your area."

The Preacher said, "This is one of the reasons that I am here. A young man was railroaded on circumstantial evidence for a crime with the same modus operandi. What I need to know is, how do I go about getting the body of the girl in this case exhumed?"

"Let me see if I can get the ball rolling, especially if it can free an innocent man. What do you expect to find, Preacher?"

"Another body of girl about the same age was found. This time they did a complete autopsy of the girl and it was found that she had been killed with a knife, like a stiletto. I believe that the first girl will exonerate Manuelo Bustamante based on new evidence found. I also do not trust the Sheriff. I believe that he is involved along with other businessmen. Men who are profiteering on illegal alcohol trade."

"Wow! You better watch your back, Preacher, as they say. You have my word that I will work with you in any way I can. Anything else I can do for you?"

"Yes, you have a federal agent who is here working on a missing persons case and also works for the treasury department, do you know him?"

"I do, he is a good man and can be trusted. As a federal agent, he has more access to information than I do."

The Preacher said, "I'm glad that I came and grateful

for what God is doing in the lives of those who believe in His Son, Jesus Christ."

"Padre, before you leave, would you do me the honor of going to dinner with me. I know an Italian restaurant here in town. The owners are two of the nicest people you will ever meet."

The Preacher said that he had to go to the newspaper office, which would take about a half hour to look up some information concerning a piece of property. He needs to see the selling price for the area. He also wants to verify if an autopsy is mentioned about the young woman found in the woods. "I suppose I can after I get done with the research. It's now after three. I should be back by four. Is this okay with you?"

"Sounds great to me, Padre. See you in an hour."

The Preacher went to the newspaper building. He saw a sign that said where the old newspapers were stored. The office was located in the basement. The building had been constructed in 1878, and was listed as one of California's Historical Landmark. It was constructed of thousands of bricks and smelled musty. He stopped as he almost passed the room. He opened the door and saw a tall willowy woman who greeted him hello. She was dressed in a long black dress and wore her hair in a bun. Her nose was similar to Ichabod Crain, long and thin with a bump on top. Her long bony arms stretched out of the sleeve. As she smiled her demeanor changed as if she had been transformed from an ugly duckling into a gentile soft looking woman. She greeted the Preacher with a soft throaty voice.

"Hello, Reverend. What may I help you with?"

The Preacher said, "God bless you. May I ask how do you work down here? It seems very hot."

"It does get very hot in the middle of summer, but with the fans all working, a few windows opened, and a fan in my office, I manage. I suppose I'm used to working here after twenty years."

"My name is Pastor Leonardo Flynn. I'm new in this part of the country and I need to see some old newspapers about two years ago. That deals with a missing young woman whose body was recently found."

She said, "I know exactly the case. Let me get the papers." She came back in about five minutes with four or five news articles pertaining to the missing girl.

"Thanks," he said. He found what he was looking for as he memorized some of the men's, faces and name of those interviewed. He thanked the woman by her name, Laura.

She said, "How do you know my name?"

The Preacher said, "I thought of someone you reminded me of. A dear friend named Laura."

"Sir before you go will you answer a question, when is our Lord coming back? I'm a Christian woman and teach Sunday School at our local church. My students are always asking me."

"Tell them what Jesus said; in Acts 1:7 (KJV) *'No one knows the time or season'* I am sure you will handle it well. See you again soon.

The Preacher looked at the large clock that stood across the way on the corner which read 3:40 PM. He decided that he would ask the federal agent if he knew the price of acreage in the area. He started back to the court house and saw Agent Smith standing at the top of the entrance to the court house talking to a young couple with a small child. As he approached the agent and the couple, he noticed that they were involved in a lively discussion regarding prohibition.

Agent Smith was against any and all types of alcohol, but the young man felt that wine should be allowed based on the history of the vineyards in California. He felt sorry for the growers that lost a lot of their income due to alcohol being banned. They both turned around and saw the Preacher approaching them.

The Preacher smiled as he said, "I hope I'm not interrupting a private conversation."

Agent Smith responded, "Certainly not, Preacher. This is Harry and Patricia Lang. They own a vineyard not far from here. They are having a rough time because they grow mostly wine grapes. It has become difficult for many growers because they have had to replace one type of grape for another – table grapes. It takes a few years before the vines start producing fruit, so in the interim, they have to look for outlets to sell their grapes for plain grape juice which has become highly competitive, thus the price of grapes has almost destroyed the industry. What do you think Preacher?"

"What I think? It is difficult to answer. My personal feelings are based on what scripture teaches us. Christ and His disciples drank wine, a naturally fermented wine. Unfortunately, there are those who are predisposed to becoming alcoholics. In other cultures, the people drink wine instead of milk or water. They seem to deal with using wine as it was intended. It is also used in alkali water to reduce the salt, and is still being used in the near East today to make the water drinkable. The Roman soldiers along with Paul the Apostle used it this way. As for alcoholism being discussed, I'm afraid it will have to be saved for another time. I'm running on a tight schedule."

The couple said, "Goodbye, and we would like to hear more."

He gave them his phone number in Cambria when they left.

Agent Smith said, "Are you ready for a great Italian meal? It's a block down the street owned by a wonderful couple, Tony and Nina DeAngelo. You will love them right off when you meet them. Let's go."

It took about five minutes to reach the café. As they walked inside, they heard a male voice say, "Signore Smith, what a pleasure to see you, and who is your friend?"

"Tony, this is a minister from Cambria, Preacher Flynn."

The Preacher said, "It is my pleasure Mr. DeAngelo"

"Please call me Tony, and this is my wife, Nina. Please both of you sit over near the window. Let me fix you the house specialty. I know you will like it."

As Nina brought some antipasto and fresh Italian bread, Tony said, "Please eat it. It will take a few minutes to prepare the main course. I saw your picture in the paper and saw what they said about you. I am honored that you came to my home since we live in the back of the café. Can I get you some coffee or a soda? As you know, we are not allowed to sell wine anymore, but the food will make up for the lack of wine."

The Preacher said, "Let me ask God's blessing on the food. He thanked God for the meal and asked God to bless Tony and Nina in a new business. They were thinking about buying another restaurant."

Tony said, "How you know I want to expand business?"

"God told me as I was praying and said that someday you would own a chain of fine Italian diners."

Nina came back to the table with an Italian seafood soup called Cioppino. They sat in silence for about ten minutes enjoying the great taste of the food.

The Preacher broke the silence by saying, "You were right! Fantastic dish, similar to a Spanish dish my mother made on occasion called Seven Mares."

As they were almost finished eating, the Preacher glanced at the clock on the wall as it said five thirty. He told Agent Smith that he had a few minutes until his bus came and said to Tony and Nina that the food was fantastic. "I have to catch the 6:00 PM bus to Cambria. I have about fifteen minutes. Again, thank you all for a wonderful meal. Remember what I told you; if you believe in God, what I said to you will happen. Goodbye and the Lord's blessings upon you and your family."

It took him about ten minutes to he reaches his destination just as the bus was turning into the terminal and walked over to the front door. Jake opened the door. He stepped back as the bus emptied out and had to wait a few minutes.

Finally, Jake said, "Hi, Preacher. Did you take care of all your business?"

"I sure did and had one of the best meals I've had in a long time. I met the Italian couple who own the restaurant. Fantastic food! I had a bowl of the house specialty called Cioppino. It's a little messy, but delicious. How about you, Jake? Have any problems?"

"No, Padre. I'm still walking on a cloud. It's the first time my back hasn't hurt since I got wounded in France. Excuse me, sir, I need to announce our return to Cambria. Hope to see you in church this Sunday."

"Look forward to seeing you and your family."

The Preacher walked to the back of the bus so that he could observe the riders when a young woman sat down next to him.

"Is this seat occupied?"

"No, it's not," he responded. "The bus filled up very quickly."

"It's Friday, and it's this way each week. People going home for the weekend. What about you, sir? Do you live in Cambria?"

"Yes, I recently took over the Cambria Church as the minister."

"So, you are a Preacher. How do you like living close to the ocean? Summer and spring are very beautiful; you can't beat it."

He paused for a couple of minutes and thought of the first minute he saw her. He knew that she was a call girl, then he spoke to her. "Nancy, when are you going to quit grieving your husband and two children? You have been carrying the load instead of letting Jesus Christ do it for you. You can't bring them back, and selling your body to ease your pain is never a solution. There are a lot of women who lost their husbands in the war. Your husband and two children drowned in a horrible accident when they were caught in a storm. The sailboat was not geared for rough seas and capsized. They were not taken from you for only God knows why. Your husband was on leave, ready to go over to France and the accident took them."

By this time, tears were running down her cheeks as the mascara compounded the expression. She grabbed the Preacher's arm and started to rail him as she said, "What right do." She got no further when she buried her head in her hands and gently sobbed for about five minutes.

The Preacher said to her, "Why don't you ask Christ to forgive you? He will start the healing process."

"She said, "I don't know how. Will you show me?"

"Yes, Nancy; I will. Please repeat after me: Dear Jesus, with all my heart I ask your forgiveness for all my actions these past nine years. I pledge that I will try to live my life as a woman of God. I ask your forgiveness for all my sins."

As she repeated these words, he could see the Holy Spirit cleansing her heart. Even her face had a beautiful smile. She was a new creation and a born again Christian. The Preacher had given her his handkerchief as she wiped her tears, and joy filled her wounded heart. God gave her a new heart filled with the Love of Jesus.

"You are a new creation. You must develop a prayer life so that you can know what God wants from you daily. Read the scriptures. A good place to start is in the Gospel of John. Come to church on Wednesday evening. Get acquainted with other single men and women. If the church doesn't have a group, start one. You have others that are praying for you to develop maturity in Christ."

They chatted, and then she said, "Pastor, can I ask you a question?"

"By all means. What do you want to know?"

"How did you know that I was having sex for hire?"

"When I first saw you, you reminded me of the story of Jesus in the Gospel of John chapter eight, when a woman was caught in adultery. The religious leaders brought her to our loving Lord. He knew what they were up to. He turned the tables on the accusers by saying to the multitude *'You who are without sin cast the first stone.'* (John 8:7a JKV) He never gave up on her, a sinner, and neither has He given up on you; but for some people, they carry their own guilt which shows on their faces. As Jesus said to the woman, *'Go! And don't sin anymore.'* I say this to you, because he has given you a second chance in life. I also know that in the future you will meet a Christian man who will fill your needs and you his. When you meet him, you will know that he is the one. That's all I can tell you now. One more thing, concerning you and your mother, she has never stopped praying for you since you left in anger. She will welcome you with a love you have never experienced from her. She gave her heart to Christ a few years after you left. I hope to see you in fellow ship with her this Sunday."

They both sat in silence when Jake yelled out, "Cambria last stop for today. Next bus at 6:AM, and second bus to Paso 10:00 AM tomorrow. Thank you for riding with us today. Have a great evening." They both said goodbye to one another.

Jake came over to where the Preacher was standing, thanking the Lord for adding a new believer to His flock. "What do you need Jake? Is there something that I can help you with?"

"I wanted to thank you for the miracle that you did."

"Jake don't thank me but thank Christ the Lord for your healing, and that your name is written in the Lambs' Book of Life. Hope you can make it this Sunday along with your wife and family."

"I called home from Santa Maria and told her how you had prayed for me, and what God did through you. She is all excited about being in church this coming Sunday. She said that she has never been baptized and would like to if at all possible"

"I would be honored, but frankly, I don't know if there is a baptistery in the Church. If not, we can go to the ocean. I am committed to another couple this Sunday, but let's plan to do it the following Sunday, if that meets your schedule. There will be others, I'm sure. I'll see you in the morning. Good night."

CHAPTER 10

The Preacher woke up early, and started thinking about how the past three weeks had taxed his strength due to the pain he felt emotionally; yet he was always willing when the Lord spoke to him about specific people. He prayed that those who had committed their lives to Christ would be in fellowship this Sunday morning. He was about to go back to sleep when Little Feller jumped on top of the covers, and as usual, started licking his face. He rough-housed with him for about five minutes, then took him outside. As he walked close to the forest, he smelled a distinct smell – fire. The fire had a good start and was burning deep in the forest.

He rushed back to the parsonage and put on his pants and a shirt, then rushed out the door to the home of Deborah and her parents. Without realizing, he ran all the way and pounded on the door. Mr. Swensen opened the door and saw that it was the Preacher. He blurted out, and asked what was wrong. The Preacher told him to call the fire department and call all the volunteers from town and surrounding Cambria. Kyle and Deborah had gone away for the weekend to get to know each other again. The twins put on their clothes while Mother Swensen made the call to the local Fire Department.

Swede and the Preacher went to the shack in back of the parsonage and found some shovels and a double headed axe. They ran to the edge of the forest and approached the fire that had started in the shack where the alcohol was stored. The Forestry building was labeled, tools inside. The Preacher knew that it housed illegal alcohol. By the time they reached the clearing that surrounded the wooden building, some of the fire had sparked a few dried snags and in-turn would jump to healthy trees. Some of the men from the church showed up to help contain the fire. One of the men said that the church women were gathering food and setting up tables in back of the church. It took the fire department with water tankers for about thirty minutes to come up the dirt road that ran in back of the building. The building would explode if the fire reached the building.

The firemen and volunteers along with the church men were well over a hundred souls. They worked feverishly in getting the fire under control.

The fire Chief came over to the Preacher and said that they had the fire under control and to thank all the men from the church.

The Preacher said, "I would like to give thanks to God for the work all of the men did, all working together in unity. Thank You Lord for helping us put out the fire, and especially the Chief and his leadership in giving us instruction on how to combat a fire. We also thank you that no one was injured. We give thanks to You, oh, Lord God. Gentlemen, we have a church gathering waiting for us and praying for us. I'm told that the ladies of the church have prepared breakfast for all of us."

They reached the church and when they all appeared, the ladies and children along with some of the older men who were not able to help, stood up, and clapped for those who worked so hard to extinguish the fire. They all knew that the fire could have reached closer to the homes of some of the parishioners. The ladies also knew that those who fought the fire would need to wash up, so the church bathrooms were used.

While the men washed up, the Preacher said, "We will have church outside. After we eat, we will sing a couple of songs and welcome some new souls that are now in Gods Kingdom. Let us pray for the food." He excused himself and ran home, then he washed up and changed clothes. He went back to a hearty breakfast.

Most of the people ate in silence, a few expressed gratitude for the Lord's help in saving homes that were threatened by the fire. The Preacher heard the town clock strike 12:30 PM. He asked the people if they were comfortable having the church outside. They all said that it was a good idea. One of the men in the church was an accomplished guitarist. He was asked to play and lead the church in a few hymns. Since the hymnals were inside the church, they sang well known hymns. When they had worshiped, the Preacher looked at the crowd that was to hear his message He saw all those he had personally invited, the young call-girl and her mother, the Bustamante's, which soon would be joined by their son, Jake and his family, and the young couple who he interrupted and stopped a potential serious problem, were sitting in the front row. He gave a few announcements, especially the return of Kyle, Debora's lost husband who had amnesia for nine years. They went on a belated honeymoon at the Preachers suggestion. He also introduced those who had been healed. He said if they wanted, they could share what had happened to them. None responded to the Preacher's invitation.

"I personally want to thank a couple who was shunned by this church. Some of you stood by and let it happen, thus sharing the guilt with those who initiated the shunting. I weep for all of you that Christ died, for the very thing that some of you agreed with the Deacon Board. Shame on you! As long as I'm the minister of this church, we will follow the teaching of our Savior. Each time we judge another, you are heaping hot coals on yourself. If what I say from this pulpit and on a one-on-one, you will hear my heart. I'm going to ask all of us to pray this prayer, a prayer of forgiveness. 'Father, in the precious name of Jesus, I ask your forgiveness for my judgment of others, help me never to do this again. Amen.'"

Some of the people who were in favor of what the Board had done, got on their knees; some were weeping, and others continued praying.

The Preacher said, "Please turn to the Epistle of 1 John, Chapter one. This chapter deals with the act of forgiveness. (1 John! 1:9 KJV) *'If we confess our sins, He is just and faithful to forgive us our transgressions.'* Christ is our mediator concerning our sins. This term is a legal term. Another name used for the act that our Savior did, offering his own body at the cross as a sin offering for all our sins. The act Christ did by dying on the cross pronounced us not guilty. He, by giving his life once for our sins also made peace between us and the Father. He atoned for our transgressions before the Father. The only way to get forgiveness, is to ask Jesus our Lord for forgiveness and mean it with your body, heart and soul. He took our sins upon himself once for all, for all mankind. "God so loved the world that he gave His only begotten son." (John 3:16 KJV) Christ reconciled us to the Father. We were alienated from God and made peace with the Father. This is God's Grace at work in Christ. We read in the Gospel of John, that Christ was full of grace and truth.

There are other scriptures that use the word Grace to explain Love and Forgiveness. Earlier I reminded this church of sin that has been buried deep in our hearts. One of the reasons the Lord sent me to you was to help you repent of some of those that have been harboring unforgiveness in their soul. The Holy Spirit reminds us not to let the Sun go down on our wrath, wrath harbors all sorts of sins and surfaces when we least expect it, but Christ is always ready to forgive us our inequities.

Forgiveness is an act of a persons will, true forgiveness comes from Gods royal loyal love, imputed at the instant of our salvation. We cannot earn His love, it is a free gift from God, "poured into our hearts by the Holy Spirit." (Romans 5:5 KJV)

I am reminded of the encounters that Moses and His brother Aaron when both of them stood before Pharaoh. Nine times God hardened his heart by not letting the people leave the land of Goshen. He finally relented on the tenth time. Pharaoh realized what he had done to the Hebrews. God again stirred up Pharaoh's heart and of course, he gathered his army and went after the Israelites who had left and had a good head-start. Moses prayed to God and the Red Sea parted so that the Hebrews walked in the middle of the Sea. The Egyptians in hot pursuit took the same course as the Hebrews but, God saw Pharaoh leading his army chasing the Hebrews. He released the waters back and drowned many soldiers. We don't know how many, some say thousands, others several hundred, regardless how many, they failed to honor God and followed Pharaoh to their death. I believe that God would have forgiven Pharaoh if he would have believed Moses."

"Sin and spiritual death go hand in hand. 1 John addresses sin as darkness and God as Light. Jesus referred to Himself as the Light of the World. When we turn away from worship services we are walking in darkness. I feel remorse for people who are bigots. Their concept of salvation is like the Pharisees, they were driven by exacting laws that God did not give Moses, they changed laws to suit themselves. One example is the law of Corban. The fifth commandment is Honor thy Father and Mother, instead they gave their tithes to the temple and neglected the care of their parents, by saying I exact the law of Corban, so I do not have sufficient means for my parents. Such was some of the attitude of the rulers of Israel"

"The doors of this church shall always be open to those who are seeking redemption, how many have been turned away by self-righteous bigots. Each and every one of us was called to be a servant by our Lord, I hope we all know the story of Christ washing the disciple's feet, if you don't, I suggest you read the thirteenth chapter of the

Gospel of John. The very word Deacon means, to serve.

Today was a start, all of you who were able to fight the fire, became servants. Next Sunday we will celebrate the Lord's supper, then after our communion service we will gather at the sea shore and baptize those who have never been emersed in water. I close with one common word, spoken by our Lord in (John 13:34-35 KJV) "new commandment I give unto you, that ye love one another; as I have loved you, that ye also love one another. By this shall all *men* know that you are my disciples, if ye have love one to another" Let us close in prayer." Amen!

CHAPTER 11

After the service the Preacher went over and spoke to Manuelo and his wife Angelina. They spoke for a few minutes as the Preacher said he would go home and take a shower, and asked if three O'clock for him to come to their home?" They said that would be wonderful. They gave him instructions to their home. They left and saw Nancy and her mother standing waiting to be introduced to him. As they came over and said hello Mary McCarthy said," she wanted to be Baptized along with her mother. They chatted for a few minutes as Jake and his wife Abigail Hawkins came over to where the Preacher was drawing a small crowd. He was so gentle with them as they all said that they wanted to be Baptized. Gil and Alice also asked if they could also be emersed in water. There were others who had never been Baptized.

He called over one of the deacons Carl Turner and asked him to make a list of those who were to be Baptized. He said, "I have a list started, I figured you would need help." *As the church treasurer he felt grateful to God. He was the other Deacon that always did the head deacons bidding.* "I'll have this list for you by Wednesday at our mid- week Bible study, if that's okay with you Reverend?" The Preacher said, "Of course, I appreciate all that you do for the Lord, Carl.

He was one of the few who addressed him as Reverend. "Carl why don't you and I get together Tuesday at 5PM, at the parsonage, I have some questions to ask you about the church finances. If it's alright with you?" "I would be honored Reverend, I'll be there."

By this time all the people started leaving and saying what a wonderful sermon, as most of them felt challenged by his words. When he spoke to them, it was like he was God, not lauding it or threatening, but his love for them came from the way he spoke. He excused himself and said, "I need to go home and shower, since I have a dinner engagement."

He got home and had forgotten Little Feller, then remembered that Deborah's sons still had him and school would start soon, he was thankful to God that he filled a void in his heart and knew that he was in good hands with the twins. He showered and shaved. He also dressed in a new black suit that he had purchased.

He had earned a few dollars when he washed dishes with the money Deborah had paid him. *He thought how God always found a way for him to earn extra money for his personal needs. He also thought of an individual in the church who he felt was tied to mobsters selling bootleg whiskey. He wondered if the Sheriff was part of the mob that was trafficking both moonshine and illegal alcohol. How could he prove it without asking certain questions?* He prayed to God that he would help him in his quest to bring these men to justice. He knew two that tried to permanently cripple him.

There were also the trumped-up charges on a young man in order to hide the real motive, the young woman murdered. She stumbled upon the building that belonged to the Forest Service, filled with illegal alcohol. He thought, who was the criminal or mobsters that were the brains behind the killing and blowing up the small tug boat. A lot of questions that needed answers?

As he was about to leave for the Bustamante home, he heard someone on the front porch slip an envelope under the door. He stooped down and picked it up and opened it. Inside was a note and a thousand dollars. He read the note that said, "we know that you are poking around in our business. If you play ball with us there is more of this kind of money. If not, you are being warmed. We will contact you later for an answer. Remember we are watching you." He took the envelope and hid it in a secure place in the living room. He seldom got angry, the warning to do as they said, or buy him off, he composed himself and went to his car.

He left for the Bustamante home which took about fifteen minutes. His old car started up and away he went, asking God for some answers to his challenge. He found their home as they had directed and was met at the door by Angelina with a beautiful smile. She was a very attractive woman with jet black hair with a streak of white in her hair. She had green eyes that sparkled when she spoke. She was a small slender woman with light brown skin. She had a way of speaking that showed an inner strength. She ushered the Preacher into the small living room, very clean with family pictures on the walls and furniture that was well worn but clean. The table was all set up with all sorts of homemade Mexican food. The Preacher loved Mexican food, that came from his mother's cooking, especially the tamales and the hot steaming tortillas. They sat down to eat and Manuelo asked the Preacher to ask God's blessings for the food.

Angelina said, "I hope you will like the soup, it is Tortilla soup, my own recipe. I use chicken in broth, add spices to the stock with a light red Chile and of course the fried Corn Tortillas." The Preacher said, "It is absolutely fantastic." After the first spoon full. When they had finished the first course, she brought out a dish that the Preacher had only tasted, Pollo in Mole. A Mexican dish made with red Chile, and chocolate and peanuts and ripe bananas. She also served hot corn tortillas or flour homemade. She had also served Mexican fried rice a special recipe she used, passed on from her grandmother and a plate of refried beans. When they had finished eating, she served a Spanish desert called Flan, topped of, with a cup of Mexican coffee with canella and milk.

When they finished eating the Preacher said to Angelina, "Senora you are a marvel at cooking comida Mexicana, why don't you start a Mexican restaurant here in Cambria, perhaps the restaurant owned by Deborah, would be willing to work out something. If you are interested, I will speak with Deborah when she returns and see what she has to say."

"Two other issues that are very important, the purchase of the old farm that belongs to the Swensen's. Mr. Swensen is asking a fair price, for the entire farm. The land and the small house are included in the price and he is willing to carry the loan, at no interest. If I were you Manuelo, I would contact him right away, and if you wish, I can be with you when you talk to him about purchasing the property? The other subject has to do with your son. I am working to see if they will exhume the body of the girl and do an autopsy as to the cause of death. I will be hearing from an agent who is trying to get the county coroner to do his job. That's all the news I have. One thing more, we need to keep praying that those who are involved will be exposed and brought to justice. I also want to thank you both for being so gracious in attending church this morning, and thank you for one of the best meals I have ever eaten gracias, al Senior."

"I have had a busy day and I am tired, so if you will allow me to pray for you and your great hospitality, I will excuse myself and hope to see you when you make an appointment with Mr. Swensen. God bless Manuelo and Angelina, thank you Father for bringing them into my life. Give them good health and strength and a speedy reconciliation with their son. Thank you for a wonderful afternoon, Amen."

They came over to the Preacher and hugged him and sent him home with most of the leftovers. He was thinking of an old hymn he sang years ago, "Blessed Assurance" as he made his way home. When he arrived at home there was an individual that he knew would be highly upset, the head deacon. George Cain was sitting on the steps of the parsonage. The Preacher spoke first; good evening, George I have been expecting you, I know that you are a busy man with all the property you have and know that you are over extended monetarily in your business. I also know that your wife has threatened to leave you and return to her parents, along with your three children. Is this part of what you want to talk about with me, or should I get you to admit that because you are tied in with the Mobsters? Laundering money and getting a cut from the Bootleg-Money. Shall I go on George and add that the woman who you are having an affair with has threatened to expose you to the authorities."

By this time George was shaking all over and sweating profusely, on top of this he had been told to lose weight because of his high blood pressure. He blurted out, "who told you all this about my private life, you had better watch out. I have some friends that you don't want to meet. I came here to let you know that you can't dismiss me without a vote from the assembly and a full vote from the Deacon board. That's why I am here." The Preacher responded, "do you want me to expose you to the entire church, that you have been spending church money to pay back some of your debt."

George said, "how dare you threaten me." "George, I'm trying to save your soul, but the state of mind you are in, you need to ask God for forgiveness. I suggest you go find a place and pray to God for forgiveness. There is no forgiveness without repentance, George, you ask how I know about your private life, it was revealed to me by the Holy Spirit."

With this, George took off in anger. The Preacher began to weep for George as he made his way to his bed room and undressed.

He lay in bed as his thoughts went back to our Lord on the night He was betrayed how he handled it, by saying to Judas, do what you have to do. Sleep set in as he drifted off.

He awoke at his usual hour six am and laid in bed for a few minutes. He felt well rested and went into the bathroom, shaved then took a quick shower. He thought about his encounter with George Cain. *He thought he felt sorrowful about how this man had ruined his life with an appetite for alcohol and loose women along with a penchant for gambling. He thought about his wife and children, as he had noticed that they were missing at yesterday's services. She had made her threats real, she packed up and left with her children. He had abused her physically and on one occasion had broken her arm. If only he would listen to sound council, but perhaps it was being shell-shocked during the war, or raised by wealthy parents that had different moral values themselves.*

Just as he finished putting on his shoe's he heard a knock at the door. He went to the door and saw a somber face staring at him. It was a member of the church who blurted out, "I'm sorry to disturb you Reverend, but I have some bad news. Some fishermen found George Caine dead on the beach this morning, about an hour ago. The Coroner was called along with the Sheriff, they just got there, so the Sheriff asked me to fetch you. He wants you to come as soon as you can."

"I can, but first do me a favor and contact the other Deacons of the church and tell them I will meet them at the same place where the men of the tug boat blew up and sank."

The Preacher took off at a fast pace as the young man named Robert. He parted at the corner where the café was. It took the Preacher less than twenty minutes to get to the place where they found Georges remains. He saw the Sheriff talking to a crowd of people, as he approached the crowd, along with the Sheriff and the Coroner. The Sheriff had tried his best to preserve the area incase George's demise was not of normal causes. Soon, two of the church Deacons arrived. Swensen and Charles McBride, the other two were not contacted because they work in Paso Robles.

The Sheriff came over to the three men, the Preacher and the Deacons. "Sorry to have to meet in such sad circumstances, the demise of George." The Sheriff turned to the Preacher and asked him, "Reverend, when was the last time you saw Mr. Cain?" "I saw him last night when I got home from the Bustamante's. He was waiting for me sitting on the porch. It was obvious that he had been drinking when he tried to speak, he slurred his words. I felt that his anger and condition which he was in, that he should not be driving. I tried to advise him as I felt he needed to step down as the head deacon. I told him that his private life was not becoming a man in leadership in God's Kingdom. When he left screaming saying that he had friends who could take care of me. It was about 9:30 PM last night when he left. I went right to bed since I was tired due to a very long day. I had just taken a shower this morning when a young man from the church, brought me the sad news."

The Sheriff said, "what about you two gentlemen, can both of you, account for your actions last night?" Each of the two men had provable alibis. The Sheriff said that he wanted them to be available. The coroner had finished his initial examination, he said; that it looked like he died by drowning, but I will have the results in a couple of days, after I have completed a full autopsy." The Preacher was listening intently to what the coroner was saying, but his eye caught sight of the mobster, Guardino. He was standing outside of the small bait shop, about a hundred yards from where the Preacher was standing.

The Preacher said, "Sheriff, I was informed by an agent of the government that Mr. Cain was on the take from the Bootleggers, is there any truth to this? of The Sheriff was taken aback by the candor of the Preacher, as he said, "That's utter nonsense. I've known George for 15 years, and believe he was a man of moral character. I demand that you tell me who the agent is so I can notify his superiors." "Sir, I reveled a sacred trust as a minister by even mentioning that George Cain had a drinking problem, but the autopsy will bear me out, by the condition of his liver, am I not right Mr. Coroner?" "Sheriff, the Preacher is correct, acute alcoholism can be determined also by jaundice, noticeable in the white of the eyes and color of the skin, which has a yellowish color." At this point the Sheriff said he had some pressing business to attend too and left to find his car. The preacher noticed that Guardino was walking towards the Sheriff and stopped him from getting into his car. They stood talking to each other for a few minutes, then they both left. The Preacher knew that his suspicions were correct. The Sheriff was involved with the Mob. He thought how unfortunate that when people lose sight of God and follow a shallow path, becomes a wide road, a road that leads to destruction. He also wondered if the coroner was also involved in the sale and transporting of illegal alcohol, most of it stolen. Moonshiners were also involved. He knew who the Moonshiners were, he thought, there would soon be a day of reckoning.

He started to excuse himself to the two deacons, then thought he should ask them to join him at the parsonage for some breakfast, but Mr. Swensen said, "no, you come to my house for a good breakfast cooked by my wife. Dan

Cartwright, who excused himself due to a commitment. The Preacher went with Swede in his car, which took about five minutes. They both entered the house and Little Feller saw him and jumped all over the Preacher. The twins were winding down summer and would soon be back in school. The Preacher was thankful to God for placing the boys in a position of caring for Little Feller. The Preacher missed him not being around, so he promised to himself that he would spend more time with him. He thought, one day he would have to leave. Mother Swensen met her husband at the door and said, "tell me all about what happened to George Cain." He told her he would while they were eating.

They sat down to eat and she poured each one of them a steaming cup of coffee; she smiled and said, "ham and eggs with freshly made biscuits and country fried potatoes." It took about ten minutes when she came in with a steaming plate of eggs a slab of ham and country fried potatoes and a pan of hot homemade biscuits. She said "if you want some gravy, you will have to wait till next time. While she served herself, she asked about George and what had transpired. Swede filled her in as to what had happened to George Cain. He said, "that Martin Grady the Sheriff asked a lot of questions of the Reverend, but the Reverend was quick to respond that threw the Sheriff off of his little game of manipulating those he feels threaten by. The Preacher had all the right answers. I learned some things that I didn't know. We will know more the cause of death when the coroner has completed his autopsy.

The Preacher decided to interject some light on the subject as he said, "I would hope that the people asking about what happened to George, should be cautious about sharing on speculation. Discretion should be followed in sharing information. People have a tendency to dramatize accidents and traumatic incidences. I know you are both very kind and generous, but we must protect George's family. His wife left him because of some family issues that needed to be resolved. We should strive to protect his wife and children and other family members. I have information that I will eventually release. Of all the people I have met, you are truly my brother and sister in Christ."

"What have you heard from Deborah and Kyle?" "She called yesterday evening. She is so excited to rekindle Godly love with her husband. They were sweethearts in High school. Kyle is struggling with his role as the head of the family. When he left for war, she was pregnant with the twins, now that he is home, they are still a shock to him. They are nine years old, when he left, they were not born. He missed all of their formative years. This is one of the issues she is worried about."

The Preacher said, "I need to make a suggestion, the military has specialist for men who are suffering trauma, amnesia is one of many. It won't cost either of you any money, and with the help of the Lord he will recover, but it takes time."

'I have another subject that needs to be addressed, a replacement for George, it has to be the entire Deacon Board decision. Swede will you set up a meeting for next week, not this week because we need to give the family time to make arrangements and a date when we can have a memorial service for George. We know that somewhere along the way, he lost sight of serving God first, not himself. I did not know him in a personal manner and if I could have saved him some grief, I would have tried harder."

"Swede, I need to talk with you and your wife about a private matter. I am acting as go between for the Bustamante's. They came to me about a piece of property they wanted to see if they could purchase. I asked Deborah who the owner was, "she said, that you owned the Property. That the total price included the small house." "Reverend, before you go any further, my daughter told me that they were interested in the property. I started praying that I could work something out for them, you were an answer to my prayers. Mother Swensen and I are willing to work out an affordable plan for them. I will contact them today and see what we can work out." "That's great, I'll let you work it out with them."

"As your pastor, I think, you have been keeping the church above water, due to the missing funds, am I right?" "Yes Reverend, I did not want the church to have to file for bankruptcy." The Preacher asked, "how much money is missing?" Swede answered, "I discovered the theft by accident when a friend of mine who works for a utility company called me and asked me why the utility bills were not being paid? I told him I would check it out. When I went over the outstanding bills, the amount is close to eight thousand dollars from the missions' fund and the general fund." The Preacher asked, "how he found out how much was missing" How did you know that the funds were missing, or as you say stolen?" "I was glad I could help the Lords Church. I think you know who stole the money." The Preacher asked, "One question, don't we have a church treasurer?" "No, George always counted the money. I found several IOUs that George, had written. By this time, he had taken about fifteen hundred dollars, and most of the General fund had a steady trail of theft, even the money that we had set apart for the Widows and Orphans, this was the largest amount that he had stolen."

"I told George that if he didn't stop taking church money, I would expose him and take-over the church bank accounts. With what I put in, and the number of tithes, we are still in the red, about eighteen hundred dollars. I figure we will be in the black in a couple of months." The Preacher said, "Thank you Swede for being so candid and truthful. One day I will tell you how I knew that George was trying to lead two lives. Scripture tells us that you cannot serve two masters, money and God. George chose Mammon. We will have to tell the other deacons what has transpired. Is there anything you want to ask me?"

Swede said, "I don't know how to put this but, people from the church would like to know more about you and have the same question I asked. Where do you get your information about people and your energy is amazing? "The preacher responded, one day you will find out. I need one favor."

"I need a small stipend about fifty dollars, for some personal money for clothing and other personal needs. I was thinking fifty dollars a month to start with since you pay all my home expenses, I think this is fair." "Reverend you amaze me, if we can't pay you more a month, we should close the doors to the church, I will guarantee you will get your monthly wages." "Ok thank you, the Preacher said." Swede said, thank you for the love you have for God's sheep.' The Preacher said, "Let us pray for the things we discussed and thank God for His guidance." As the finished praying. Amen!

After they prayed, the Preacher called Little Feller and he came running as he walked out of the home of the

Swensen's.

It was a late summer, warm afternoon. He decided to take a walk in the forest. After strolling along for about an hour. he found himself near the place where they found the remains of the murdered girl. He found a stick and dug around dirt and fallen leaves. He found some signs left by the authorities.

As the Sun's afternoons rays showed their brilliance through a small clearing. As he admired the Suns-Rays, his eye caught a glitter of an object. He walked over to where he saw the object as he stooped down for a closer inspection. It was a metal object partially uncovered. He soon uncovered the entire object it was a long stiletto knife. It had some spots on the blade, only an expert could determine what they were. He pulled his handkerchief from his pants pocket and wrapped it so that no one could say it was contaminated as evidence. He looked around for a large enough rock to protect the place where he found the stiletto. He found just what he was looking for and covered the spot. He then decided to go back and call agent Snowden and tell him what he had found.

The officer in charge was already in Cambria because of George's death. The secretary said," he would be calling in about an hour." He told her to tell the agent, that he would be home. He also said it was urgent. She said she would pass the information on.

It took the Preacher about twenty minutes to walk home. When he arrived, he made a pot of coffee and had a Mexican Pie called an Empanada. He sat at his little kitchen table and started thinking back to when he arrived. *He thought of the pain and hurt to many of his current flock caused by misguided souls. Each church member and some new converts had been exposed to sin by those who once were honest, God-fearing people. He thought, where did they go wrong and lose faith with the Lord. It doesn't take much, as he remembered what happened to Moses when he struck the rock in anger.* The Bible says that he lost faith by being angry. He had angered God. Moses was not allowed to enter the promised land. God took him to the top of Mount Nebo and showed him what he had missed.

His mind drifted back to the two years he spent working in the fields with Mexican farm workers. He especially remembered the camp fire gatherings at night as he recalled the sound of guitars playing gospel music, some in Spanish and some in English. There was a brotherhood built between the different cultures and races. He cherished those memories. They would remain in his heart for life and he was saddened that it had come to an end.

He thought there were so many loving moments, when he had to deliver a baby in one of the camps. He remembered the woman by the name Gloria Sanchez and her husband Domingo, they had other children, unfortunately the baby was being delivered breach, but with the help of another older woman named Teresa, sent by God to help deliver a healthy baby boy. He remembered how many times he had to go to the county jails and intercede for men who have had too much wine to drink, but we were able to get them released to me as an itinerant Minister. Tears came to his eyes as he had to obey God. He was sent to set things right in the Cambria Christian Church. He was brought back to reality when he heard a knocking at his door.

CHAPTER 12

He went to answer the door and their stood Gil Snowden, "come on in Gil, want some coffee and a Mexican Sweat Bread?" "Sounds like it might be a delightful sweetbread." "It's a Mexican pie. You can get them with Chile meat and beans or you can get them with apples or sweet potato, it's called an empanada. I know you will like these since they are home made by Mrs. Bustamante."

"She is the mother of the young man held for a murder he did not commit. She sent me home with a large care package." After the second one eaten by the Agent, he sat back and said, "man where did you get these, I have never tasted any-thing better, in Mexican Food." "I'm glad you like them. The reason I called you is I found the knife that I believe killed the Girl. I found it after church yesterday about fifteen feet, from the spot where we found the body."

"Let me walk you back. I went for a walk in the woods, a ritual I have practiced since I arrived in Cambria. I found myself near the spot where the missing young women's remains were found. A few feet away I saw a glitter from the Sun, shining on a small piece of metal, like a piece of glass. When I stooped down, I found what looked like some form of metal. I dug around the object, it turned out that it was what is called a stiletto. I immediately used my handkerchief and wrapped it in the handkerchief, thinking it could be the weapon that was used to take the life of the young woman, that's why I called you. I personally believe it is, but can't prove it until we get permission to exhume the body."

"Wow, I have one question. Did you secure the spot where you found the stiletto?" "Yes, I placed a large flat rock and marked it with certain scratch marking." "You are thinking of the same thug, Tony Guardino, known to kill with this weapon." "I, wanted a professional opinion so I called you thinking it might be part of your jurisdiction' "I am glad you did; do you have the weapon in your possession.?" "Yes; I do, let me get it for you, it's in the bedroom in a safe place, under a certain painting, come with me and I'll show to you."

They went to the bedroom to a drawing of our Lord Jesus Christ, below is a table with a loose floor board. Under the board is where it is safe. "Let me get it for you, as he lifted the floor board and pulled out a brown bag, inside was the stiletto. Agent Townsend was very careful as he pulled the weapon from the bag. "The first thing he noticed was a decolorization on the blade, which he surmised it was blood. He also felt that there could be fingerprints that would bring the killer to justice." "He said to the Preacher, "if this is the murder weapon, it can get Mr. Guardino the Electric chair. We might have a hard time getting a district attorney to get it approved as exhibit one. Do you mind if I call the Sheriff and get it into his hands?" "The Preacher said, "I have a hard time with Sheriff Mathew Brady, I have felt from the first day I met him that he is involved with the Bootleggers, and with the death of the girl."

"May I ask Reverend, why you feel this way." "No, I don't mind. My first encounter with him was when I helped save the four men when the Tug Boat exploded. I felt he questioned me about the cargo. that He was trying to involve me in some way. He was more concerned about the loss of all the bottles, rather than ask me about the survivors. This morning when I was summoned by him to identify the body of George Cain, he started to interrogate me. I told him that I barely knew the man. I had only spoken with him three times. After they took the remains of George to the Morgue, I happened to see Tony Guardino out of the corner of my eye walking towards the Sheriff's patrol car. He stopped and had what seemed from where I was standing, they knew each other."

"Reverend; rather than take the Stiletto to the Sheriff I will take it to the State DA. I know I can trust him, since we have worked a couple of cases together. If you don't mind, would you take me to the spot where you found the evidence." "Agent Snowden I would be more than happy too." Snowden said, "I have a camera that I carry in my car, if you are ready, let's go. We don't have much daylight left."

They made good time to the spot. The agent took pictures with a flash attachment in order to give more light. *The Preacher thought someday someone would design a camera without a need for a light. To develop they need to be able to speed up the time and light reflector. He was no expert on cameras but he knew enough about light and darkness.* Just as he was about to say something, he heard a rifle shot. He dove behind the log and stayed calm. Agent Snowden cried out, "hit the deck," as he also dove behind the same log. As the shots continued, they heard rapid firing, while they lay on the ground. Feller had been with them. So, the Preacher whistled for Little Feller, he came running and ran over to the Preacher and lay still. The Preacher could feel his little Heart beating. The agent had pulled his revolver and was trying to get a fix on who was firing at them.

They could hear noise in the woods as the firing had stopped. The agent said, "I have a fix on where the shots came from. Reverend; please stay here with the dog, I will come back when I'm sure where the shooter or shooters are. If you hear more firing, stay put. The culprits may be waiting on us to show ourselves." The Preacher said a prayer of protection for the agent as It seemed that he had been gone a long time, but felt relief when he heard a voice say, "Reverend it's me Gil, "I'm ok. I spotted two men, maybe fifty yards from where I was laying. I heard them running, so I tried to chase them, but they had a car parked on the dirt road. They were hollering at each other for missing us with their rifle shots. I doubled back as the car drove out of sight. I was able to get the license plate number, Calif 8763. I also found three shell casings 40/50 crag we had better head for the parsonage. Let's go, as the agent said, it's getting dark and we can't do anything more here."

They returned to the parsonage as they were opening the door, when the Preacher said, "I don't know about you but I'm hungry, it's almost six thirty. I have enough Mexican food in the ice box that Angelina Bustamante gave me to take home with me yesterday." "Agent Snowden replied, "now that you mention it, I am too, I love Mexican food." The Preacher said, "Ok, it will take a few minutes to warm the food in the oven, it depends if I can get it to work. I have never used one before, but with the help of the Lord, it will work." He retrieved a long match as he turned the gas on and to his glee it started, he adjusted the temperature gauge. It was a few minutes when the Preacher took the food out of the oven, he placed the food on the table, it was enough for four people; he turned to Gil and said, "let's eat."

The Preacher made a pot of coffee, as they chatted for a few minutes until the coffee was done. The Preacher placed the Pollo in Mole, rice, beans into a bowl. He heated the tortilla soup on the stove top. He had wrapped the corn and flour tortillas in a slightly wet dishtowel. Placed them on the table. The Preacher gave thanks for the food."

They sat in silence until they were almost done and completely satisfied, and of course feeling stuffed. The Preacher said to Gil, did you like the food? He said, "I have never eaten such tasty Mexican food in my life. It was awesome, when you see Mrs. Bustamante, thank her for me." "I Sure will, as a matter of fact, I have to see them in the morning, why don't you thank her yourself?" "Good, I'll go with you. Tomorrow is Tuesday, my schedule is clear."

"Gil, why don't you camp out here. You can sleep on the couch, unless you have a room in one of the hotels we have here in Cambria?" "Reverend, thank you for the offer, but I'm staying here in a Cambria hotel, which is only a couple of blocks away. I have some phone calls to make in the early morning, and I really need to shower and put on some fresh clothes."

"I need to get going, it's nearly ten O'clock. I'll say

goodnight and look forward to meeting the lady who is such a fantastic cook." He walked out into cool night air. The Preacher called for Little Feller as he came running into the Living room. As he did the Preacher reached down and picked him up. They had both bonded to each other. The small animal had been his companion for less than a month. *The Preacher was in a melancholy mood. He thought how lonely a man can feel when the woman of his life dies before him. He thought what a lonely road he had been assigned to by* God. He then came back to his senses, as he wiped a tear from his eye.

He opened the door, and singled for Little Feller to follow him to take his normal late evening walk. He thought to himself that he should walk on the main street of Cambria. Ever on the alert when he didn't know the community. He suddenly stopped, sensing that there was danger. He called for Little Feller to come to him, always obedient to his master he came running from behind a bush. He jumped into the Preachers arms as a couple of tough looking characters came from the bush. He recognized them as the two brother moonshiners. The Preacher always ready to react when in danger, said. "Stop right there before you come any closer. I will give you two choices, one you can continue and try what you have in mind, to kill me, or you can ask God for forgiveness and save your souls. One more thing, you will find hell a horrible place to spend eternity.

The Bible tells us that you will know you are in hell as your sins will be shown to you, for eternity."

I'll Give you a couple of minutes to make up your minds. Me personally, I would love to see you both in church this next Sunday. My message will be on forgiveness; you need a touch of grace from God." They both stood in their tracks, mesmerized by the words flowing from the Preachers heart, guided by the Holy Spirit.

As he stepped closer, he continued as he went forward, both men fell prostrated, on the ground. The Preacher put his hands on the two men as they begged God for forgiveness. Both men lay on the ground for several minutes, then they slowly got to their feet. The first question they asked him, "who was the man that said to us, "I forgive you of your sins, as he showed us all the bad things we ever did. He also said that he died for us. Our father died at the hands of a government alcohol agent when we were nine and ten years old. We started to hate everyone until you came to town. We want to tell you that we didn't kill that girl that you and your pooch found. We will be in church this Sunday Reverend, and again thank you for showing us where we were headed."

"This is hard for us to say, but our mom read the scriptures to us when we were growing up, until pop was killed, she changed so much after his death, all we heard from there on was, there was no God. She also died of alcoholism, at age fifty." The Preacher went over to them and hugged each one assuring them that God loved them, that He died and rose on the third day for our sins. We are going to Baptize this Sunday come prepared to get dunked after the services. See you both Sunday; as he walked back to the Parsonage.

He had locked the door with his key, but when he arrived, he noticed that the lights were off. He distinctly remembered that he had left them on. He wondered what awaited him as he reached for the living room light. There on the couch was a familiar face. He said, it's been a long time Roberto how did you open the door without a key? It's been a couple of years since I last saw you. Let me think, ah yes it was in Arizona during the melon season. You left in such a huff, and mad at me and the world. I am glad to see you, but I'm not sure why you are here?"

"Leonardo, I have been looking for you to ask your forgiveness. After serving a year in the county Jail in Yuma I started looking for you. While I was in Jail, I did a lot of thinking. One day, one of the inmates had a Bible. I started to read the Gospel of John. The owner of the Bible was released. He gave me the Bible.

I continued to read it and soon found myself studying it. I would go back and read a verse, then asked myself if it applied to me? In many instances it did. One day while sitting in my cell trying to read by the light outside the cell, I heard a voice that said to me. Roberto, it's about time for you to ask Me to come into your life for eternity. At this point I realized it was God talking. I fell on my knees and started weeping. I kept asking for forgiveness when I suddenly stopped. My quest came to an end after all the years I was searching for God, but He found me."

"When I was a young boy in New Mexico I worked with the shepherds caring for their flocks. Then I read the part in John where it talks about Jesus is the good Shepherd and my sheep hear my voice. At that moment I thought about you and wondered where you were? One day I was finally released from jail. I went looking for you because of what the Bible says about asking your brothers forgiveness. I went to all the places we had picked fruit together and remembered what you thought us about forgiveness and loving your brother. By accident I picked up a Newspaper and saw a story about a Preacher who saved four men from drowning, and of course it gave your name, Leonardo Flynn. It gave the town as Cambria California."

"Here I am; I want to ask your humble forgiveness for what I put you through. I took the drugs I was using and placed them in your Knapsack, of course when the Cops came into the camp and started looking through our belongings. I thought I was not going to be found out because they didn't find them in my Knapsack as well as yours. I had forgotten that I had one joint in my shirt pocket. One of the cops looked in my shirt pocket. When they looked at you, something about that look in your eyes made them afraid to search your knapsack. I believe that the people who you ministered too would have stood by you and say they saw me place them in your sack. When I went to jail, I received a two-year sentence, but because I only had one joint and had no record, the judge cut the sentence to one year. I got out about a year ago, so here I am, again with all my heart I ask your forgiveness."

"What you have related to me and to see you here how could I not believe your sincerity, of course I forgive you. Oh my, it's almost midnight and we have talked without me asking you if you want a cup of coffee and, ah let me see if I have more empanadas, he looked in the Icebox and found two, as he said great, I found two. After heating the oven, they sat in the kitchen drinking coffee and eating the Mexican meat pies and reliving old times they had worked in the fields together.

The time was two thirty when they went to bed after a time of prayer Roberto slept on the couch and was fast asleep as his head hit the pillow. The Preacher thought about the scripture that Paul wrote, in (Romans 8:28KJV)

"And we know that all things work together for good, to those who love God, to those who are the called according to His purpose." Soon, the Preacher was deep in his sleep, feeling secure and dreaming of a better life in Christ.

The Preacher was startled as he heard the sound of a frying pan on the stove, and the aroma of fried potatoes and onions, with the smell of freshly brewing coffee, caused him to sit up in bed. He realized that Roberto was in the kitchen cooking up a fine Mexican breakfast.

The Preacher got up and went into the kitchen, and said, "good morning, Roberto, how did you sleep?" "I was up before the Sun came up, so I decided to cook us breakfast. I looked at what you had in the kitchen and all you had was potatoes and eggs. So, I'm making a torta, out of fried spuds, unions and Chile, mixed and poured into a pie pan, then baked in the oven. I found some tortillas which are a little dry. then I cut them in pieces placed the other increments, on top. Added some salsa then placed in the oven, until the eggs are fully cooked. Then you cut the Torta like a pie. I call it a Mexican quiche, without cheese. It will be ready in about ten minutes." The Preacher said, "I'll set the table." "Ok Pastor, I hope you are hungry. Oh; I also took your mut for his morning walk, he is in his basket taking his morning siesta."

After the food was ready, they sat down to eat. The

Preacher asked Roberto, "what are your plans for now, you mentioned that you would like to share the word of God, with the Campesinos and other field workers. I encourage you to go for it, but it is a lonely road, cold nights, sometime having to sleep in barns and being stopped by law enforcement and asked where are your credentials, also being spit at, cussed at, at times beaten, robbed and even thrown into jail. It is the loneliest road you can choose. Paul the Apostle describes what he went through because he was a fallower of Christ. You should read Second Corinthians 11:16ff. He was beheaded for being a follower of Christ. There are many believers who feel God has called them into full time ministry, but find themselves broken, because they would not take counsel from a mature Christian."

"Not all those who are called into ministry have a Damascus Rood experience, like Saul of Tarsus. Some see or hear men preach the Word, like Billy Sunday, or Spurgeon. Just to name a couple of Evangelist. Because of loneliness some men turn to the use of alcohol, or choose the dark side by doing immoral acts with women. A few become pedophiles. These are just a few things that some have suffered. One way to know if you have been called to full time ministry, is a feeling of something you have to say about Christ, a burning sensation inside. Godly men and women will confirm the call, usually two or more. If you are still not sure, there are those who have the gift of

Knowledge, you will know them by what they say and how they communicate God's call."

"Pastor; I believe that what you have said to me is sound counsel. Do you have a word for me from the Lord?" "I will pray about what you have told me. My heart is glad that you desire to preach, but ministry carries other standards, especially in your private life. If you get married, how do you and your wife respond to each other. When children are involved, how will you raise them according to God's standards for fathers. How the community sees you is also important? I suggest that you read 1 Timothy chapter three. Paul wrote the guide lines for those who Christ selects for full time ministry." Roberto sat there as if he had been slugged with a sledge hammer, then he spoke up, "in other words you don't think I'm ready to start out on my own?" The Preacher asked, "how old are you, Roberto?" "Does my age make a difference? I'm twenty-two."

"Do you know what the word maturity means, in a Biblical sense?" "I suppose I don't, I'm starting to believe that it takes years to be able to preach or teach." "It doesn't take years, but a desire to serve. Jesus our Lord had twelve disciples, yet he spent three years living and nurturing them until he felt that they were mature enough to send them out on their own.

No one knows how old the Apostles were, but Bible

Scholler's say that they were a mixture from barely out of their teens to about late forties, they were mature in the ways of God, because they spent those years very intimately with our Lord. They ate together, slept wherever their trek took them. Then our Lord felt it was time to go to the cross. I don't know for sure I will be here in Cambria long enough to prepare you. Only the Lord knows how long. I will be here."

"I'll tell you what I can do, I almost forgot you didn't say how long you would be staying in Cambria, what are your plans?" Roberto said, "I was kind of playing it by ear, but after what you shared with me, I feel, I had better pray to the Lord and ask for guidance."

The Preacher said, "I think that is a wise decision Roberto, one more question; how far did you get in school?" "Reverend, I only made it to the tenth grade." The Preacher said, "a time is coming when you will have to have a Master's degree from a Seminary, or a reputable bible school. You should go to night school and take the courses you lack, so you can express yourself, this is a gift from God, the Holy Spirits anointing to teach and preach. There are some men who have gone into the ministry without being licensed, a handful were successful in leading people to Christ, but most of them drop out and don't want to spend the time under another older mature minister. I hope what I have told you about ministry does not discourage you.

The Preacher said, "I repeat to you that it is a lonely road for an Itinerant Preacher, why do you think Jesus sent his disciples in pairs. Paul and Barnaba's, also took along John Mark on their missionary journey. John Mark, was Peters nephew. He became discouraged so he decided that the work was difficult. Paul and Barnabas split because they disputed John Mark's willingness to suffer some of the situations Paul described in Second Corinthians."

"You have to decide what your gift is. There are five ministries described by Paul in Ephesians chapter four. Apostles, Prophets, Evangelist Pastors and Teachers. My understanding of this passage of scripture is that each are a gift from Christ to the church so they can teach the members of the Lord. These men are equipped to teach the scriptures of Christ to all until we attain the unity of our faith, this is maturity."

"Roberto, I don't know where you are in your knowledge of the scriptures, but I'm going to give you a small challenge, by reading the entire book of Ephesians, and when you have read it, I will give you a short quiz. You have two days to study it, Ok."

"Reverend you are a tough teacher when it comes to doing the Lord's work." "Roberto, I am very cautious about the sacred writings of God. I am also looking out for your spiritual welfare. Think about what I have been saying to you."

The Preacher continued, "I have an appointment with a couple in about an hour, you can stay here if you want too, pray and ask God what He wants you to do, and please read the book of Ephesians. I have to get dressed, and thanks for fixing breakfast." The Preacher went into the bathroom and showered, shaved, then to his bedroom and dressed. Just as he finished there was a knock at the door, it was Snowden, right on time. He quickly introduced him to Roberto then they left.

"How did you sleep last night Reverend?" He said, "not bad considering I stayed up late until around three am reminiscing about the times we worked in the fields following the crops, especially when we got through at night and sat around a fire, and ate our dinners. Then we would sing songs, Spanish folk songs, some Christian one's and a few Negro spiritual song's. A few had guitars, or a mandolin, or once in a while, someone would show up with a Banjo or Harmonica. It was open to any who could sing, especially the spiritual ones. It was a beautiful time of interacting with each other, yet all from different racial backgrounds.

Young or old or in between, we were united by the Lord's music. These were the good times, and bad ones on occasion. The one thing that brought us together I believe was the Holy Spirit. It was rare when someone stepped out of line, because of me they always wanted to hear Bible stories, some scriptures and a closing prayer. How about you Gil, did you sleep alright?" "I did after talking on the phone with my wife, for about an hour. After she hung-up I went right to sleep. I awoke this morning to the sound of somebody singing, a woman with the voice like an angel, I asked the desk clerk who was doing the singing? The guy gave me such a look, I thought I had used profanity in his presence," then he said, "mister you said you heard a woman with a beautiful voice. No such woman exists here but every so often we get someone who heard the woman. It's always the same voice and the same melodic sounds." "He said some other strange things, have been going on for almost a decade." "At this point I turned in my key and told him I had to go since I had an appointment to keep. That's how my morning went."

"Interesting what you told me Gil. In the Mexican culture there is a mythical woman called la Llorona; kids sit around camp fires and talk about her crying. Thus, you get the name Llorona. Some say she is crying for her lost children, others for her lover. I have always felt that it was started by some parent to try and scare their children when they misbehaved, perhaps what you heard was a real woman, but she may have been warning you to watch out, for she may visit you again. Just kidding Gil. Some say it is a demon, others a fallen-angel other's a mythical character. I will you let you decide for yourself, besides we are here," as they pulled into the driveway.

They walked up the stone pathway and were about to knock on the door when Manuelo opened the door and said, "Angelina and I were expecting you. Who is the young man with you?" The Preacher said, "let me introduce you to Gilbert Snowden a friend of mine. He works for the federal government and is here on another case." Manuelo and Angelina said, "It is our pleasure senior, a friend of the Pastor is always welcome in our home. He is helping us purchase a piece of land. We are happy to report that Mr. Swensen sold us the property, yesterday and he will carry the note at no interest. The land and the house he sold to us for eight thousand dollars. We saved for years and had over five thousand dollars in the bank. We gave the first installment. We will make payments each month of a hundred twenty dollars, till paid in full. He said I can work the land now and move into the house. Angelina is going to talk with Deborah when she comes back from vacation, about being a cook. El Senior He take care of us, and we appreciate what you do for us. Have you eaten breakfast?" "Yes, we have said the Preacher, but Angelina we would love a cup of your coffee and un pan dulce." "Bueno, I will fix for you."

She was gone for about ten minutes. The Preacher said, "can we sit at your table, there is more that I want to share with you about Manuelo Jr. I brought Gil with me because he feels like you, that your son was wrongly charged. We both feel that you can't bring charges against your son because he said hello to the murder victim. An honest DA would not have brought charges against your son. We have contacted the California Sate District Attorney's office because we recently found a weapon that we believe is the weapon that killed the girl. Before we can get a new trial, they have to exhume the body as well. The Sheriff and the county district attorney were in a hurry to get a quick conviction and the attorney that defended your son was incompetent. It was his first case and he was not equipped to represent your son. We should hear something by Monday of next week. I have been wanting to go visit your son, maybe I can go see him Saturday."

Gil said, "I can go with you if you don't mind. I have convinced my boss to let me work on both cases, since we believe, they are connected to our other problem." The Preacher said, "Sounds great to me Gil, we will have to leave fairly early. Why don't we go up in the morning and stay overnight and come back Saturday? Do you know any hotels close to San Quinten?" Gil said, "I do, and I will call when we get back to your home and make reservations for two." The Preacher said, "Ok, it's all set then. Manuleo and

Angelina we have to go, Jesus taught that if we love God everything will work out for good if we have faith, and trust Him."

It was close to noon when they got back to the parsonage. When he walked into the house, he knew that Roberto had left. The Preacher found a note on the kitchen table from him. "Dear pastor, I want to thank you for the counsel you gave me concerning ministry. I don't feel that I am ready, but I will take your advice and go back to school and finish High School. I'm going home to Texas where my family is. They live in the town of Lubbock. I can get a job and go to night school. I will drop you a line when I get home, besides I haven't seen my mom in over a year. I also have a girlfriend that lives close to my mother's home. I have a son that I haven't seen in almost three years, and besides I need to make it right and marry Carlotta. I hope to see you someday, Roberto. P.S I will send you my address when I get home. God bless you and your ministry."

Gil said "why are you crying Reverend?" "I'll tell you in the morning, besides I have an appointment later today and I need to spend some time getting ready for today. See you early in the morning, about seven, Ok." Gil nodded, ok."

CHAPTER 13

The Preacher opened his eyes as he awoke from a sound sleep. The week had started with a lot of excitement and here it was Friday. He expected Gil to show up early, he should get up right away. He looked at the clock which read, five thirty. He quickly made a pot of coffee and took a shower while it was brewing. He finished his shower and shave and put on his clothes.

He took Little Feller for a short walk then returned to the parsonage. He noticed a fairly new Packard thru the window, parked in front. A great riding vehicle. He would drop Little Feller at the Swensen home. He felt rather guilty not being able to spend more time with him, but you could see that he liked the affection the twins gave him, plus all the people the Preacher knew, but liked the boys the best.

He went to the front door and called out to Gil to come in and have a quick cup of coffee and a sweet roll that he had bought a few days ago, unfortunately they were a bit dry and hard. He knew a trick that he learned from the women in the fields. Wrap them in a slightly wet towel and steam them for a few minutes, they will taste like they are freshly made.

The Preacher said, "sit down for a few minutes. Let's drink our coffee and eat the rolls. Then we can leave, I have to drop Little Feller off at the Swensen's, if that's ok with you?" "No problem, Reverend, I was able to get us a room with two beds, if that's all right with you?" "Of course, grab a seat and sit please. How many hours do you think it will take for us to get to the Hotel in San Francisco?" "Gil answered, the way I figure, between six and a half to eight hours. It's six AM right now, do the math. From here we drive to Paso Robles, about an hour and a half, onto Highway 101. Then about a hundred and sixty miles to our destination." The Preacher said, "Ok, sounds like a good plan. Let's get going.?" Gil answered, "were on our way." They put Little Feller in the car drove the block and a half to the Swensen's. The Preacher took Little Feller inside, after five minutes, he came out in a hurry and said to Gil, "let's, go."

They were in luck, the road working crews had finished the section of road that had been under repair for a couple of months. They finally arrived at the end of the road. The sign read, left to San Francisco 161 miles. They decided to stop at a coffee shop and us the restroom. They were back on the road within twenty minutes.

The next town was King City, nestled next to the

Salinas River, called the upside-down river, because it runs from South to North. The San Antonio Mission, is about an hour away. They had to stop for gas in King City. Back on the road they came to Salinas, California, not far from Carmel. Gil said, "let's stop in Salinas for a sandwich and a soda." They spotted a sign that read, Coffee Shop next exit. They turned right on the next road and saw the café. After ordering a sandwich and a glass of root beer they ate their lunch in haste, used the rest room then back on the road again. They drove for the next three hours until they reached the outskirts of San Francisco.

They still had to go to Marine County, then to the Prison, the oldest prison in California founded in 1852. Manuelo Bustamante Jr was in one of the cell blocks, they could see him for questioning for his crime only. Gil Snowden Federal agent used his leverage to get in to see him. After seeing the Warden, he was very cordial, wanting to please the Government. After walking to the cell block, they were allowed into a private room where they could converse with Manny as he liked to be called. Gil introduced himself then the Preacher. "My pleasure to meet you."

"Manny my name is Leonardo Flynn, as Gil said I'm here on behalf of your parents. When I arrived at Cambria, I met your folks and they told me an outrages tale how they were treated when you were wrongly accused of murder.

Since then, we have been working with the State District Attorney, we found what we believe is the weapon that killed the girl, but they have to exhume the body, because the coroner failed to do a proper autopsy. The DA is working on getting a Federal Judge to intervene. We want to ask you a couple of questions regarding why they charged you with the crime. Tell us everything you remember about the first time you saw or met the girl?"

"The first time I saw her was on the beach in the early afternoon. She was sitting on the sand near where I was studying for an entrance exam to a university, as a pre- med student, California at Berkeley. I will have to find work if I am accepted. To answer your question, as I told the authorities that it was the only time, I had ever seen her or even knew she existed. After she went missing, they said that someone had seen me walk away with her. After I left the beach, I remember she smiled at me when I left. The next thing I know they are charging me with her killing. I never saw her again until I read in a newspaper article who she was and saw her picture. That is everything I know about why I am in prison. I pledge on my love for Jesus Christ my Lord and Savior, that all I said to that girl was hi."

The Preacher reached over and gave Manny a big Christian hug, and said, "son I believe you and see how flimsy a case they have. I want to assure you that I believe you will be given a new trial and released right away, but you must be patient." "Reverend, my folks wrote me a letter mentioning you, my trust is in God and I know that you are a man of God. My time in prison has not been unfruitful, I have been studying the Bible every day and studying medical books here in the prison library." Gil added, "I have known the Reverend for a couple of weeks, but I assure you that he will do everything within the Law to clear you. Certain people abused you by not giving you a proper lawyer and a proper trial. I will assist him in any way I can to free you, and if I know the state DA, he will not rest till he sees you set free."

Many said, "I trust in the good Lord as the scriptures teach us. I was in prayer the other day, and I heard the Lord say to me that I would be released soon, and to be patient. For many years I have wanted to be a doctor, but I feel that God wants me to go into the ministry. He said that He would confirm it with a man of God. The Bible says that all things must be confirmed in the mouth of two to three witnesses, does this make sense to you Reverend?" "Yes, it does Manny. On the way here the Lord spoke to me to anoint you with oil. He said that you were a chosen vessel of His. It will be confirmed by two others, besides myself. Please kneel on the floor and repeat this simple prayer. Heavenly Father I surrender my Life to you and to whatever ministry you call me too. I will endeavor to follow the code of a Shepherd-overseer's conduct in 1Timothy chapter three. I promise to try and see human beings as Jesus sees us, sinners, but full of grace and Your love. I pledge this with all my heart and soul and body, mind and will, remembering that I am a servant not to be served, but to serve others. Thank you for being my Shepherd. Amen."

The Preacher said, "we must go Manny, but remember well these words, God loves you and what he desires is that you love and obey Him with all your heart, give me a hug we must go." As he motioned to Gil to follow him out they called for the guard and said, "we will see you soon Manny!"

As they walked to the warden's office, they had to walk through a couple of cell blocks. The normal thing for most inmates when free people pass their cells they whistle and yell obscenities at those who are visiting death row. One of the guards said in a loud and commanding voice, "don't you know who one of the visitors is, he is a minister a priest or Padre, treat him with respect. Some of the cons yelled out, "sorry Preacher we didn't know."

As they approached the Wardens office, he came out to the foyer. He asked if Manny was in good spirits, as the Preacher responded by saying, "he has a great outlook on life and who he serves, God. He is a fine young man." "Reverend and agent Snowden, I have some great news for you both. I just got off the phone with the State Attorney's office and they are reviewing the case. They have given permission to exhume the body and accept the stiletto as the murder weapon. On closer examination they found excellent legible prints on the knife. They will have everything needed to reopen the case and exonerate the young man. I'm sorry that I didn't get the phone call earlier, but they say that the wheels of justice work slow, if you don't mind, I will tell Manny after dinner." "Thank you, Warden, for keeping us up to date on Manny's case, we look to the day he is reunited with his parents. Are you ready Gil, let's go and find our hotel, and a place to eat dinner?" Gil said, "the hotel has a dining room so we can eat there."

It took about twenty-five minutes for them to find the hotel and get an open parking spot. They had forgotten that it was Friday. People in San Francisco like to eat out, especially on the weekends. After checking in they went to their room and placed their bags on their respective beds.

It was around seven in the evening. They each had to use the restroom and freshen their faces. They went to the coffee shop of the hotel and were shown their table. It was a medium size dining area. They sat next to a large window and started looking at the menu; the Friday Special was a Prime Rib dinner a baked potato and a salad, hot baked rolls and desert, along with a drink of your choice, all for $2:95 Tip not included.

"Reverend the dinner is on me, do you have a preference, I'm going to try the Prime Rib." "Sounds good to me, and for a drink I'll have a cup of coffee after we finish, that will be two orders of the same." As the waiter came to take their order, he said what will be your choice?" "Gil said; two orders of the special." "It's my pleasure sir, thank you for dinning and staying at the Palace."

After the waiter left the preacher said, "does the Government pay for all your expenses when you are on the road?" "Yes, they do and I am allowed so much a month to take someone out for dinner and two nights' maximum for a hotel." "Are you tired Gil?" "Yes, a little, but I'll be ready to return to Cambria, it's such a quaint community. It's a shame it is a hot bed for illegal alcohol. Reverend do you think they will vote to abolish the law of prohibition? What does the Bible say about alcohol?"

"Gil, I believe that to restrict the use of all alcohol, considering the drinking of wine is not prohibited in the Scriptures, along with beer in some countries and cultures it is served with meals. Alcohol in moderation, especially wine from the days of Noah. When he stepped of the Ark, he planted a vineyard then when the grapes were ripe, he made wine. When it was ready for consumption, he drank it and got drunk and passed out then laid down in his tent, and when one of his sons came in and saw his father naked, he exposed himself in a manner that caused him to curse his grandson, Canaan."

"Paul the apostle wrote to Timothy to drink a little wine for his stomach. Solomon In the Book of Proverbs states, '" *It is* not for kings, O Lemuel, *it is* not for kings to drink wine; nor for prince's strong drink: Lest they drink, and forget the law, and pervert the judgment of any of the afflicted. Give strong drink unto him that is ready to perish, and wine unto those that be of heavy hearts. Let him drink, and forget his poverty, and remember his misery no more." (Proverbs 31:4-7 KJV). "My understanding of this passage of scripture is, dealing with Hebrews who were very ill, and suffering much pain or they were dying. It was to help him feel better. This has been a hotly heated discussion among Christian denominations. I go along with Paul and his writings. He uses a good argument by stating that if wine or meat causes another to stumble then the one who has a problem drinking in moderation, then he sees another brother drinking, he may think it is alright. Then the one who drinks should abstain. If we were traveling to other countries where Christian's drink wine with their meal, then its ok to drink when it is served with your meal. I say drink in moderation."

"As to Prohibition, I feel it will be rescinded by a new president in a few years. When you prohibit an adult to abstain from a culture that has been in existence for thousands of years, you will have a problem, any type of alcohol. People will soon make their own, or purchase illegal bootleg booze. Then moonshiners come into play. I hope this clarifies part of man's mind set in drinking alcohol."

Gil said, "thank you for the small teaching, but the law currently on the books, has created a problem as a law. Alcohol consumption in some countries is a magnitude of great proportions creating a new class of citizens. One of the side effects affecting society and the church, is the breakup of the home. There is another heart-breaking tragedy. One, the abuse of alcohol, is the rise of broken homes, along with the effects on their children. Miss guiding children by role modeling, that its ok to drink hard liquor. In the eighteenth-century England had a tremendous rise in the abuse of Gin, affecting many women."

When I worked with the migrant workers, I saw a large percentage of the men who looked forward to the weekend, so they could drink beer, the drink of choice. I remember a young man that was hospitalized for pancreatitis', He was twenty-six years of age, he thought that beer was non-alcoholic."

Gil said, "I hate to stop this discussion, but we need to get to bed. Look at the clock it's almost ten o-clock." Gil had already paid the bill. They made their way to their room and opened the door. Gil said, "Reverend, why don't you take your shower or bath first, I can wait till morning, if that's ok with you." The Preacher said, "Gil that's great, but are you sure? Remember you did most of the driving and some time's a good hot bath when your tired is very soothing." "Reverend you talked me into it" "Then its settled, I do need to brush my teeth if you don't mind?" "Of course not, go ahead."

"The Preacher was all set to go to bed as Gil was preparing the tub so he could soak and rest his weary body. The Preacher was praying and asking God for the ability to deal with the Sheriff when he got back to Cambria. He felt the Sherriff for some reason did not like Hispanics, and was set on keeping Manny Bustamante behind bars, but he forgot that the Preacher had the Lord on his side. He heard the clear voice from God, "My, son be patient, I have things under control. Your friend Gil is searching, give him a chance to accept Me as His God." "Thank You Father for your guidance and allowing me to be a witness for Your Son and my Savior."

He prayed for Deborah and Kyle that they rekindled the fire that had been interrupted by war. He remembered what God's word states that the trials we go through are for the testing of our faith. The Preacher felt secure that they would overcome the lost years. They would become a model Husband and Wife. He had to speak with them about Angelina Bustamante cooking Mexican food, which would be an asset to them. You could have special Mexican dishes or American food. They can hire her and try her for a month. He would offer them this proposal. Gil finally finished his bath, then into bed. Then both said good night and soon they were sound asleep.

CHAPTER 14

The alarm went off at six AM. They both jumped out of bed. Gil used the facilities first. He shaved and then dressed, as the Preacher showered, shaved then dressed. The Preacher asked Gil to see what time it was. Gil responded; "Reverend it's five minutes after seven. How soon will you be finished dressing?" "Give me about five more minutes and I will be ready to eat a sweet roll and a cup of coffee. Why don't you go down to the restaurant and order for me? I would sure appreciate it." "No problem, I'll see you downstairs. I suggest that you bring your bag with you so we can leave right after we eat." "Good, I won't be far behind you."

The Preacher finished putting on his shoes, grabbed his duffel bag and found Gil sitting at a table drinking a cup of coffee, waiting for a Bear-claw, as the Preacher said, "how did you sleep last night?" Gil said, "ok, in fact I didn't wake up during the night, how about you?" "I usually don't sleep well when I'm on the road, but last night was a rare night, I slept like a baby. Here comes the waitress with our Bear claws and another cup of coffee for you Gil." After both had their second cup of coffee Gil looked at his watch and said, "Reverend we better get on the road It's almost eight, being Saturday, I don't know how the traffic will be. They got up from the table and headed for the parking lot.

They made their way to where Packard was parked. the attendant, came over as the Preacher paid the fifty cents for all night parking and soon were on their way.

They had to maneuver the streets of San Francisco till they saw a sign that said, Salinas fifty miles. They sat and drove in silence, until Gil spoke-up, "Preacher I need to ask you about something that has been nagging me, what does the term "Born Again" mean?" "A great question Gil, first and foremost, it is scripture, Jesus our Lord in the Gospel of John chapter three. A Pharisee by the name of Nikodemus came to Jesus in the night for fear of the Jews. He had heard about Christ and the healing and teachings. He made a statement to our Lord no man can do the things he does that only God can do, note the answer that our Lord used. (John 3:2-3 KJV) Jesus answered and said unto him, Verily, verily, I say unto thee, except a man be born again, he cannot see the kingdom of God." The beauty of this scripture is a clarification of how we enter into Heaven.

When He said in, (John 14:6 KJV) "I am the way the truth and the life. No one The only way into my kingdom is to believe that He is God incarnate. Gil do you own a Bible? If you, do I recommend that you read the entire book of John, but in chapter three Jesus gives us insight to what Born Again means, he is not saying to enter into your mother's womb again."

"The entire book of John gives us a word picture of the deity of Christ. In other scriptures He solidifies His deity by stating that He and the Father are one. Gil, I have a question for you, I sense that you have never asked Christ into your life, Am I right?" "Reverend, I have never, that's why I asked you the question, being Born Again." "You answered what I thought, that you were not born again. Why not ask Christ into your life, no better time than right now, I can pull over to the side of the road at the first pull-out we see." "Yes Reverend, I believe I have seen how you deal with people, with complete strangers. You treat them all the same, but always with a tenderness in your heart. Theirs a pull-out coming up."

Gil pulled over onto the side of the road. The Preacher said, "Gilbert Snowden, have you listened to everything I have said about being born again? Before you answer, I have one more important thing. Giving your heart to Christ will not change your environment, meaning the daily things of life will not change, but you will change from inside. What you do right now, is that your priorities will change to God's priorities. Placing Him and others first."

The Preacher said, "this is the start of being a servant.

Now, say the sinner's prayer, repeat after me. Heavenly Father forgive me for all my sins that I have committed in my life, I ask you to forgive me and ask that You and Christ take over my life as long as I live on this earth. Lord I believe what the Holy Scriptures teach, that Christ died for those sins and that He rose again on the third day. He will come again in the future. I promise to obey you according to what Your word tells us to do. I will try to always keep You first in all my daily chores. I will make errors, mistakes and sin knowingly and unknowingly, but because of your grace I remain saved. I thank you from the bottom of my heart for my salvation. Amen!"

By this time, Gil was crying tears of Joy. The Preacher said to him, "from this day forward you are a new creation, but the challenge to you will be to spend time in reading His word and praying, it is a must. God's blessing to you and to your wife for all the prayers she has prayed to the Lord for your salvation."

Let me drive so you can focus on what it means to be, Born Again. I was going to ask you and your wife to come to the church so that I can Baptize you. I know she will be proud of you, as a special favor to me, let me Know when you can attend. I don't know where you live, but you can stay with me at the parsonage and sleep in my bed, I can bunk on the couch. We should get going, it is almost noon and we are just coming into Salinas, which is about a hundred miles to Paso Robles, then Cambria. Cambria takes about an hour and thirty minutes. Mostly because of the road conditions."

Gil, "Do you want me to continue driving or do you want to drive?" "If its ok with you Reverend? "Please keep driving. The next small community is, King City, where we can get something to eat, then you can drive Gil." "Sounds good to me, I really appreciate that you are willing to drive. I have some friends in the Agency who are not willing to drive when we are on a case, thank you for your willingness." They continued to drive in silence until they passed Salinas. Most of the towns they passed were farming towns. Spreckels sugar was in Salinas, thus the main crop was sugar beets.

The Preachers thoughts turned to Mr. Martin Brady the Sheriff. Why would a man who had earned the Medal of Honor in the Great-War get involved in bootlegging? Perhaps for a few men, killing became a way of life. Most who saw action do not discuss the battles they were in. Many who fought in the Great War, came back with their thought process changed. It unleashed the dark side of them, making and seeing crime the same as a normal way of life. He knew that the man was, killing being easy for him. If you got in his way, he would find a way to dispose of you. The Preacher had to figure a way of trapping him by his own hand.

He thought about the victories that the Lord had in using him as the vessel that touched people. He could not take the glory away from the One who died for those very sins. Tears came to his eyes as he thought about working in the fields alongside the migrants. In all his days in ministry he was never as close to the people as when he followed the pickers. He felt their pain when one of them was injured, or when they were fired because they couldn't keep up due to their age. Many had been exposed to the Sun too much and developed skin cancers, rather than complain they went back to their homes only to succumb to other diseases. Among the Negros and Mexican workers some died due to the complications of diabetes and tuberculosis.

He thought about his family, father and mother and then his wife and children. He had so many fond memories. He felt great when he was sent by God on a special assignment. His work in Cambria was almost done. There were still some issues that he had to accomplish, but time was not a problem.

He thought about his replacement that was on his way here. He was a much younger man than he was. He was also married and had one child. He almost said it out loud, but caught himself. The couple had been chosen by God at birth. He was chosen as a minister from his mother's womb.

The Preacher, also had never looked back at his calling. There were times while sleeping in the fields, that being a minister is a narrow road. He reflected on Paul the Apostle, who described his thoughts about the sufferings that haunted him, he said in one of his letters that his main worries, is the church (2 Cor.11:28 KJV) beside those things that are without, that which cometh upon me daily, the care of all the churches."

He was startled when a deer jumped the road in front of him as he had to react by hitting the brakes, missing the deer by inches. He pulled over to the side of the road as Gil awoke and said, "where are we and what happened?" "We are just passing Greenfield, we were on the outskirts of town, a deer jumped in front of us. Thank God for His intervention; we're not too far from King City, I'll let you drive when we get there, if that's ok with you?" "that's fine Reverend, let's go, as the Preacher eased the car onto the highway.

It took about thirty minutes driving when they saw a sign that read King City fifteen miles. They pulled into a Gas station to get gas at fifteen cents a gallon, normally eleven cents a gallon. They exited the car to stretch their legs, walked over to the vending machine where they paid for a Hires Root Beer. Gil said, "Preacher can I ask you a question. Have you ever felt alone in your travels?" He replied, "When I first started in full time ministry, I had to be away from home a lot, I felt all alone at times, until I met my wife. She would travel with me sometimes, these things changed when I accepted a pastorate in Lubick, Texas, unfortunately it got worse when she and my second child came along, and all three of them went to be with Jesus. I felt more alone when I sobered up. At this time the Lord clearly told me to work with the migrants. They filled the emptiness that I felt when my family died. Why do you ask me this question?"

"Let's get going, I'll tell you when we are on our way to Cambria." They reached Paso Robles. They got out of the car on the side of the highway and walked around the turn out, so that fatigue would not set in. They got back into the car and started West on Highway 46, where they would reach their destination, Cambria.

"Gil, I think I know what you were going to say. You are tired of being on the road all week long then on occasion go home to San Luis Obispo. You are tired of hotel living and on rare occasions you get to go home. I thought you lived closer than San Luis Obispo. It's only about an hour away, but you have to cover a large area, mostly North of here. As an agent being out on the field, the temptation on a man living out of a suitcase are much greater. As men we are tempted by what we see, especially a woman. Jesus in His Sermon on the Mount in one of the Ten Commandments. (Matthew 5:27 KJV) "Thou, shall not commit adultery." He changed the perspective to if a man looks at a woman with lust and intent in his heart, he is guilty of adultery. I imagine that you have been tempted?"

"My advice to you is, use your law degree, use it for its intent an attorney. Why don't you consider opening a law firm? Or perhaps go to work for a police department as a detective, or apply for the job of Sheriff. I know of one that will be available in our county, San Luis Obispo very soon. They will be taking applications for the position." Gil said, "Reverend you amaze me with your logic and knowledge. All you have told me is true. I always wanted to be an attorney, but perhaps for the wrong reasons. I read about Abraham Lincoln who was a great lawyer, and the latest is Clarence Darrow. I didn't get the offers from a major-law firms I was approached by a federal agent who offered me a job. I had to go for training, and did fairly well, but it has been a disappointment to me. I like the action and the excitement when I have to examine the crime scene. I have thought about working for the county as a Sheriff Detective, but what you just said makes sense to me. I'm going to the post office Monday and get a form and see what happens. If I get the Job, I would work out of the County Court House. We are paying for a small house. We have one child and are expecting another. I don't remember if I told you, but my wife had polio as a child and is partially crippled. She never complains. That's a brief history of my life."

"Gil, are you going home after you drop me off?" "You bet, Reverend, I want Hannah to meet you and see me baptized in the morning. Thanks for your inspiring counsel, Reverend. The Preacher said, "I'm so glad that you want her to share in His glory, as a minister It will be an honor for me to Baptize you."

"Gil, I don't know how to say what I am going to say, but straight out. It's about our current Sheriff. I have been trying to devise a plan so that he traps himself. I suspect that he is the brains behind the two deaths in the church and believe he was blackmailing our head deacon, I also have suspicions about another individual, but I won't share it with you until I'm absolutely sure. I want you to help me with a plan. I will continue to pray for both individuals. Pray about this on your way home, I know that you are a man of principle and want to see justice done. We are approaching the parsonage, thank you for all your help. Let me say a prayer for a safe journey home."

After the Preacher had been dropped off, he noticed that the restaurant was open for Saturday's special. He wondered if Deborah and Kyle were back from their honeymoon. He was tired and went straight home.

He opened the front door and saw that everything was in place as he left it yesterday. He decided to shower and change into some clean cloths. It was dark as he looked at the clock which said 6:45 PM.

He walked over to the Restaurant and saw a lot of people eating dinner. As he walked in, he saw a small table that was vacant. He sat down and knew by the smell, it was Chicken Fried steak with all the trimmings, mashed potatoes, creamed corn and a small dinner salad and roll. Coffee or tea. It said $2:00 a serving until supply lasts. He looked up and Deborah was making her way to the table. She said, "hi, stranger, how have you been, Reverend?" "I just got back from San Francisco and needed to see you and ask how your reconciliation went with Kyle?"

"It was a great time of renewal for both of us. He is at home right now with the boys, and of course Little Feller. The boys think he is their dog. What were you doing in San Francisco, if you don't mind me asking?' "Of course not, he replied. Gil the Government Agent went with me." "We went up to visit Manuelo Bustamante, He is doing fine and is in good spirits considering his circumstances, but we did receive good news; the States District attorney has received permission to exhume the body of the dead girl, because of the evidence I found; the knife. The real killer was very sloppy with his weapon. I saw an object that glistened in the sun light. I walked over to where it was partially exposed, so I dug around the object, it turned out to be a type of a knife called a stiletto, because of the length and shape of the knife. I turned it over to the State DA. They are going to exhume the body for any knife wounds found on the remains of the young woman. I'm waiting for the State Coroner to a complete the autopsy. I believe Manny will be granted a new trial and found not guilty."

"Deborah; I know that I can share a confidentiality with you. If my suspicions are clear. I believe that Sheriff Brady suppressed the truth, to shift the blame on Manny Bustamante. He was the last one to see her alive. The Sheriff had her killed by an assassin sent by the mob. The Sheriff made matters worse, by violating his oath of office, when he told the coroner to say he found nothing. This cover up indicated that someone else killed her. Manny was railroaded when he was denied due process of law. I'm sorry Deborah, I shared far too much with you, concerning this case."

"Deborah, I have a question to ask you, did your father close the deal with the Bustamante's, I guess I should ask your father, I'll see him in the morning prior to church services. Oh; I almost forgot, I was talking with Mr. and Mrs. Bustamante when I went to their home for dinner. I asked her if she would be willing to open a Mexican

Restaurant, or perhaps add Mexican food to your current menu, one day a week. Perhaps hire her as your fulltime cook. If you do, you will have to open the back room to seat more customer's. You do most of the cooking as it is, she can also cook American food as well. Pray about it and see where the Lord leads you."

"Reverend, she would be a great asset to our community. We have barely kept above water, and the people who like Mexican food, either go to Paso, or San Luis Obispo. Reverend, you have seen this place full when we have specials, the rest of the time, we break even." "Deborah; You need to talk with her about this idea. You will see her in the morning. I told her you would give her an answer. Also, let her express her ideas about food and the menu. I'm sure you will be amazed at the food she can cook." "Reverend, I will contact her this afternoon; Reverend, what is your pleasure, or do you want the special?" "No, I think I will have a bowl of Chile and beans, crackers, and a glass of milk, with a large cut of apple pie alamode, with vanilla Ice-cream. Deborah, I don't want you to think I am ungrateful. I'm not very hungry, you get enough for two meals, thank you for your concern and the care and love you have shown me, I will not forget it."

She went back to the kitchen and soon returned with his order. He sat and ate in silence. He had set the trap. He knew that her father was a friend of the Sheriff. He asked God to intercede if his suspicions are true. *He thought of all the lives that he personally had an impacted on this assignment. He thanked the Lord Jesus Christ to help keep him focused on why he was here.* Deborah broke his silence when she came over with his apple pie alamode. She said, "Reverend would you like another glass of milk with your pie?" "No thanks Deborah, but you can bring me a freshly brewed cup of coffee." "Coming up Preacher" As she went behind the counter where she had brewed another pot. He finished his pie alamode and his cup of coffee. He left three dollars, and waved at Deborah and signaled her that he was going home.

As he opened the door, he knew instinctively that there was an alien presence in the house. *He thought back with his first encounter with a demon. He immediately said out loud, "The lord rebukes you, Satanic force, and in the name of Jesus leave this home. The evil spirit said in a soft chilling voice, there will be another time, Lorenzo. You are being watched; this is only a warning. Oh, by the way your dog is no more."* As soon as the entity left, the lights went on.

The Preacher was startled as well, and angry that they were attacking him in his love for one of God's creatures. He felt sorrow for the loss. He thought about the twins, as to how they would react at the loss of a little mutt. He realized that our Lord could intercede in behalf of two little boys who adored the little dog. Evil is cruel without any compassion. He knelt next to his bed and asked God to spare Little Feller for the sake of the two boys. He stayed on his knees and prayed for the Swensen's, especially Mr. Swensen, who he was sure was involved with the Bootleggers, he prayed that there were other circumstances that God had not revealed to him as he prayed for the souls of the Sheriff, the Coroner, and anyone involved with the Bootleggers. He started weeping as he prayed for those who had come to love him in such a short time.

He stood up and thought about Sunday's sermon, "Forgiveness." He knew that one of the issues that caused this church to be noticed, was that they had left their first love. Love for God, Love for His people, Love for the poor and the sick, this ushered in unforgiveness and bigotry. The great war ushered in a wave of easy money, along with bigotry and legalism. The church in Cambria had become a place where money was flowing freely, caused by a flock of Christians not living by God's word. He looked at the clock, as it read a few minutes before midnight. He changed into his night clothes and then went to bed, and soon fell sound asleep.

CHAPTER 15

His alarm sounded at six AM as the Preacher awoke to a beautiful Sunday morning, he walked over to the stove picked up the coffee pot, rinsed it out and poured water enough for four cups of coffee, then he used enough coffee for the same, a special measuring spoon for coffee. He turned on the gas under the rear burner. He added the finely ground coffee. The instant he placed it on the stove, the aroma filled the house with the smell of fresh brewing coffee.

After shaving and using the facilities he poured himself a cup of coffee and took two slices of bread and placed the bread on the toaster and turned the burner on which took only a few minutes to toast. He buttered the toast and then opened a new jar of Blackberry Jam. He said his morning prayer of thanks to God providing his needs, physical, and spiritual guidance then began eating his breakfast. He had found a devotional booklet by Dight L Moody, a complete study of Proverbs. His favorite. (3:5 KJV) "Trust in the Lord with all your heart and lean not on your own understanding."

He was on his second cup of coffee, when he heard

a knock on the door. He said, "come on in, the door is unlocked." Kyle, Debora's husband walked in. Care for a cup of coffee, its freshly made coffee?" "Yes, that sounds good." The Preacher said to him, "what brings you out so early in the morning?" "Reverend I won't mince my words. It's about your little dog. Somehow, he got out last night without us knowing about it. We found him this morning close to the woods. We believe that he may have been poisoned. One of our neighbors said that their dog was poisoned last week. The boys are distraught, and blame themselves for his death. They both have been crying since early this morning. I am so sorry for the boys and for you Reverend, what more can I say?" "Don't blame yourself for his death, scripture teaches us in a very strange way, the Lord gives and he takes away, even little animals are important to God, otherwise He would not have allowed animals in the new Heaven." "Reverend do you think you can speak with the boys after church" "Absolutely, it is an honor, for all life is precious to God." "Deb and I have been talking It over and she concurs with me, that we would like to have counsel with you, say this Monday at 10." "Yes, that time will be fine. See you here in the Parsonage, ok."

The Preacher went to his bedroom and kneeled in front of his bed, which had become his prayer closet. He asked the Holy Spirit to guide him in the message He had prepared. "Love brings Reconciliation." He was deeply troubled about the demise of His little companion, today he would have to comfort two little boys who had wounded hearts. He prayed about what he had to do concerning Swede. He prayed to the Lord thanking Him for what had been revealed to him by the Holy Spirit. After he had exhausted his mind and spirit he finally said, Amen! He saw that it was almost nine, so he thought he should go to the church early. He opened the shades in the living room and saw that it was cloudy outside, so he took out his umbrella; then stepped out into a briskly morning.

He walked at a brisk pace and soon found himself walking up the few steps, of the Church. Then into a small foyer. There was a small Pastor's office and was big enough for a small group, also ideal for a board meeting. *He thought to himself; how old was the church? He would have to ask Deborah when it was first opened?* He looked inside the building and estimated it could seat up to a hundred-fifty people. *One day he said to himself there will be mega churches in large communities. Perhaps one day there would be a school in the back of the church there were over three acres of space available for growth.*

He was startled when one of the Deacons, said, "good morning, Reverend, how are you this morning?" The Preacher said, "I feel good, I was planning on baptizing people today, but it looks like rain." "Don't worry

Reverend, about the weather, it is only fog, it will lift by the time we finish fellowship.' By the way, what is your name, I know your first name but what is your Sir name?" "It's Gary Elder, but everyone calls me El. I've been in this church since I was in second, grade. My folks, or should I say my mom moved here in 1906 after the big quake, in San Francisco. I remember when it happened, it affected all those here in Cambria as well. My father left my mom for another woman shortly after we moved to Cambria. There were three of us. My oldest brother was killed in the Big War. Mom finished her education and found a job as an office helper and worked her way to top secretary for the main bank here in Cambria. While working at the bank she met a great man, who is my father. They later got married. They are both still alive and attend church here. My Mother is a strong woman of faith and made sure we were taught the Bible. She is still teaching Sunday School. My little girl is learning from Grandmother and our next child will be taught by her. We are expecting in about five months. Boy I'm sorry I banged your ear." "Don't worry Gary, how else will I get to know the people if I never speak with them. I have met a fine young man and a friend. We better go into the room. I'm sure the others are waiting."

They both walked over to the table and sat down next to each other, Gary Elder. Swede Swensen and Dan Cartwright came in, then Gus Albright. One seat was unoccupied for the man who died suddenly, George Cain. His seat would be filled by a special election.

The Preacher started the meeting, "Gentlemen; we are gathered here this morning with a heavy heart. The loss of our brother George. The circumstances that he met with his demise are still under investigation by the County Sheriff's department. We must pray for his children and wife. I would like to recommend that we meet Monday at seven pm here, we have a lot to discuss on the agenda. I hope that all of you would be in attendance. Today we need to focus on today's sermon and water Baptism at the cove. I have no idea how many will be dunked. It is Biblical. When our Lord went to visit John the Baptist at the Jordan river, Jesus came forward to be Baptized. The Baptist said, "I have need that you baptize me, but The Lord said that it was proper for Him to be baptized. (Mark 1:9-11 KJV) "And straightway coming up out of the water, he saw the heavens opened, and the Spirit like a dove descending upon him: And there came a voice from heaven, *saying,* thou art my beloved Son, in whom I am well pleased" "Water baptism has been part of the church because of what Jesus did in obedience to the Father. It is a testimony that you have received Christ into your heart. I need two volunteers to help me in the baptism?" Gary and Dan, thanks for volunteering, see me after the services this morning.

Gentlemen would you join me in prayer for the services, that God's presence would help us repent of sins committed and that people who have harbored unforgiveness in their hearts repent, a new beginning for those who are searching for the truth, Thank you Father, Amen! Oh, I want Gary to open the services as the Lord leads him and our praise and worship leader to pick the worship songs. My sermon today will deal with Love Acceptances and Forgiveness.

They all walked into the sanctuary and sat in the deacon chairs. It looked   like a king and his throne with all his subordinates sitting on the right and on the left of the Ministers seat. Deacon Elder stepped to the podium and asked the congregation to please stand for the morning prayer. After they said the morning prayer, Deacon Elder asked the praise and worship leader to lead the congregation in a couple of hymns. After they finished singing Elder asked the congregation to remain standing for the Preacher as he stepped to the podium. He opened with a prayer of thanksgiving, then he asked the church members to please be seated.

He opened by welcoming them. He said that his message was on forgiveness. He said, "please turn to the eight chapter of the Gospel of John. My sermon today is on Forgiveness, concerning the woman caught in adultery. The leaders of the temple brought her to Him in order to accuse and trap Him in what he said.

Imagine being made a spectacle because of one or more of your sins being brought forth among you in this sanctuary, to the front of the church with just a blanket wrapped around you. The main reason to shame you, then take you outside and the congregation gathered around you to stone you. There are three principals at work that I feel are important. Sin, and the act of the will, forgiveness. The leaders of the temple wanted to see what our Lord's reaction would be concerning adultery. The gospel of (Matthew 5:27 KJV) states, "if a man looks at a woman with lust in his eyes, he has committed adultery" I can hear the mob shouting and screaming to stone her. Because the law said that it was the righteous punishment. The Lord had spoken concerning the Torah, that He did not come to do away with the law, but to fulfil the Law and the Prophets.

He saw through their hypocrisy when they asked Him about the law of Moses stoning a person for a capital sin. He stooped down and was writing in the dirt, without looking up (John 8:8KJV) "he who is without sin among you let him cast the first stone." "When He said this the leaders of the temple and the crowd slowly left, starting with the eldest to the youngest, until all were gone, and left Jesus alone with the women, where are those who accused you? "She said to Jesus no one sir neither do I, condemn you, go and sin no more." (John 9-11 KJV) Christ our Lord forgave the women, when he said neither do I."

The Preacher at this juncture of his sermon looked at the congregation as He said, "I invited a handful of people that recently asked Christ into their lives. I have asked them to come forward. Each of them has a testimony of living a life against God. I welcome them to this congregation. Each person is a new creation, by asking Christ to forgive them of their sins. If you don't want to come forward that is ok, but all of you are going to be baptized after church in the ocean, a place called The Cove, but please come to the front of the church. I and the deacon board will pray with you and welcome you into this congregation.

He introduced each one and asked them to share how they came to ask Christ into their hearts. There were seven who gave a short testimony. When they were finished, the Preacher returned to the pulpit to finish his sermon. He spoke about fifteen minutes on the act of the will of the individual. Love and forgiveness and restoration, a sinner cleansed by the blood of Christ.

Unforgiveness is a selfish act of the individual because he feels that he was wronged, in many cases, but the main reason Christ came is because of reconciliation between the world and God the Father. People go to their grave who lost great rewards if they have unforgiveness in their hearts. The Preacher told the story of the prodigal son. When finished he said that they would gather at two PM, at The Cove.

He skipped the alter call after saying this to the congregation, we are all sinners, but only because of His grace, are we forgiven. He closed the meeting with a prayer of thanks. He reminded them of the Baptism this afternoon. He stepped down and motioned for Kyle and Deborah to talk with them and their sons, concerning the demise of Little Feller. They followed him into the Pastor's study along with the boys. He motioned for them to take a seat.

The Preacher said, "I hope you are all fine this morning. We lost one of God's creations who brought comfort and companionship to us. I truly loved him as you do. He will always be in our hearts with joy. God has a place in His kingdom, even dogs. Boys, I feel the same pain as you both, and will miss him. Remember him when you see someone abusing a Dog or a Cat.

"God when He created animals held Adam and Eve accountable for their care, they are in His plan for our lives. He also holds us responsible to care and nurture our animals. You both have earned respect from God and me. I will always remember how he loved you, how he reacted when he saw you. Time will heal your pain; one day you will look back at the times he brought joy to you. Perhaps, God will provide another dog for you both in the near future. Remember all life is sacred, I believe He will use you again to bring companionship to another dog. Let us pray to the Lord for peace and joy knowing that He feels our pain. The Bible says that God is the God of all comfort, so Lord I ask for your comfort as well as finding out who poisoned Littler Feller and bring that person to justice. Boys, any time you want to talk with me, you are always welcome.

He looked at the clock and saw that it was 12:10 PM. When he came out of his office there were two couples waiting to speak with him. One was Jake the Bus Driver and his wife and Gil the agent and his wife They each introduced their wives to the Preacher. Both men asked if their wives could be Baptized with them. He said they could, if they had made a commitment to Christ. Each woman said that they had given their hearts when they were ten and eleven years of age, but were never Baptized and thought it would be proper to be Baptized together. The Preacher said, "It would be an honor for me to follow custom, as shown in the Bible." Both of the women were ecstatic.

Deborah said, "why don't you all join us at our restaurant. I'm sure my mother won't mind." They all said, "sounds good to me." They all walked to the restaurant, which took a few minutes.

Mother Swensen started the grill and took out a tray of hamburger patties, she had to open two packages of buns, started the French fryer for potatoes. Deborah Jumped up and started to cut onions and sliced three tomatoes and cheese for those who wanted a Cheeseburger instead. Within twenty minutes they were eating their burgers and fries.

The Preacher asked Deborah and Kyle if they had thought over the idea of offering Mexican food along with their regular menu. She said that her father and mother were all for the change. They had been losing more money, barely able to make their payroll. She and Kyle were also in agreement. All that's left is get Angelina and Manuelo to agree.

They would make posters and get the local newspaper to run an add. They were excited about the entire venture. Manuelo and Angelina would be in town to meet with the Preacher along with Kyle and Deborah.

The Preacher looked up to the clock and said to those who were being Baptized, "folks we need to get going." They all got up and thanked the Swensen's for the Noon meal and said they would be along shortly. The Preacher rode with Gil and his wife, a trip that took five minutes. They found a parking spot close to the tackle shop and from there they walked to the sandy beach. There was an old shack that people used to change clothes, and behind the shack was the outhouse.

When Gil's wife exited the car, she needed help. She had to walk with crutches. *The Preacher thought to Himself; "Lord please restore this young woman's crippled legs. I know that she is a wonderful woman by the way she loves her husband, you have heard her prayers. I know that she is a prayer warier. It would be a great testimony for you and for the skeptics as a witness to them. I always try to do your will Father, and give you the honor and the glory."* He was startled back to reality, When Gil said, "Preacher look at the crowd from the church. It looks like all of them came to see, in support of those being Baptized." "Gil, I never expected to see such a crowd, but they will see God's power and glory today, I pray that there are those who are searching for the truth, will give their hearts to Christ"

The Preacher had changed into old clothes and walked down to the water. Those who were being baptized had on white gowns. He counted 18 people who were waiting. The Preacher was standing in the water along with the two Deacons who were helping him in the ceremony. He stopped and faced the congregants and said, "I want to thank you all for coming on such a joyous occasion, I am blessed to be able to serve you as a minister of the Gospel. I have a saying that fits us all. God has called us to be Soldiers of Faith, Messengers of Hope and Ambassadors of Love. My prayer is that we all live up to this little prayer that spells out what God expects of all His servants. First thing, I want you to do, all the singles who are being Baptized, please make a single line. Then the couples and the last couple is the Snowden's for a special reason."

He started immersing the singles and then the couples. They finally arrived to Gil and his wife Sarah. He spent a few minutes with Sarah and Gil, then He asked her, "do you believe that Jesus can restore your legs?" "Yes, I do with all my heart. I have been praying for years, I believe that this is the time." The Preacher said, "Let us see His power at work and that He will heal a woman crippled from childhood. Lord we pray in the name of our Lord Jesus Christ that this woman will be healed."

As he immersed her in the water he said, "I Baptize you in the Name of the Father, and the Son and the Holy Spirit." He brought her back up and behold her legs were straitened, as she stood crying and calling upon the name of Jesus, as she kept thanking Him. As she came out of the water all the people said that they had seen a miracle of God. The Preacher also thanked the Lord for his prayer being answered.

He fell to His knees and wept while others were thanking God for what He had done. A great number came and asked the Preacher to intercede for them for forgiveness and asked for a re-commitment. After asking God to forgive each of their sins. When he had finished praying a cloud burst opened as It started to rain. Most of people ran for cover, others just stood on the beach and kept thanking God for His Majesty and Omnipotence. After about a half hour of a heavy rain it stopped and then the Sun came out and a large Rainbow shown over the water, as if God were blessing them all.

Deborah and Kyle invited everyone to the restaurant for coffee. As they left to open the door and put on a large pot. Some of the people had made other plans, especially those with children went home, but some of those who had been Baptized came and sat down at the tables. Deborah stood up and said, "let us go into the back room where we can move tables together. All, wanted to sit near the Preacher. They sat down waiting while the coffee finished perking. Deborah and Mother Swensen and a couple of other women helped to serve. They also had a large selection of cookies.

Gil and Sarah sat next to the Preacher. The others asked all sorts of questions about divine healing. The Preacher decided to speak to the subject. He said, "let me clarify some myths about divine healing. The day of Pentecost is described very clearly. When all the Apostles gathered in the upper room. They were in prayer, when a mighty wind came upon them, tongues of fire. The Holy Spirit Baptized all of those present with some of Gods power, for the sole purpose, to give his anointing power for the work of service. This also is the day that the Christian church was birthed. The book of Acts gives a picture of what happened over nineteen hundred years ago."

"We read in scripture about the gifts of the Spirit found in 1Corinthians chapter 12-14. Let me back up. Shortly after the outpouring of the Holy Spirit, Peter stood up and preached a message of salvation. Several thousand received Christ as their Savior and were Baptized with the Holy Spirit.

Shortly after this John and Peter were going to the Temple where they encounter a man who was lame from birth, in front begging for money. The two disciples stopped and said, we don't have any money, but what we do have, in the name of Jesus the Christ, rise and be healed.' When Peter said these words, the fellow jumped up with his legs and ankles healed and ran into the Temple leaping and praising God." The Preacher said, "The Bible doesn't say how many people were saved because of this man. Divine Healing is God's grace in action."

"Unfortunately, people have made a mockery of Divine Healing, by holding revivals about Healing. Jesus, never had to hold revivals, He preached the Gospel. Paul the Apostle is clear as he wrote in (1 Corinthians 12:11 KJV). "But all these worketh that one and the selfsame Spirit, dividing to every man severally as he will." "Dear ones, because of the time, and has been a long day what we witnessed was the power of God. I suggest that you read 1 Corinthians Chapter's 12-14. I do get tired and this week has been a very tiring week for me. By the look on your faces, you concur. Good I will mark that in my memory bank. Before I explain the verse as I understand it. I want to clarify that it is the Holy Spirit who anoints a person with whichever of the nine spiritual gifts. He heals those He deems appropriate at that moment for His reason. It's only when He wills.

"God has always healed when it Glorifies Him. You will hear of various places where people were healed, and some miraculous healing took place. I have been asked why we don't have a record so many healings done. Some glorify themselves. When Christ was empowered by the Holy Spirit is what you witnessed today. Sarah's healing was to Glorify the Father."

"I have heard men say that they feel healing in their hands. We should never test the Holy Spirit, to do his bidding. The only spirit they worship is, the spirit of self. These are the false prophets Jesus Christ our Lord warned us about. The Gospel is a gift from God, we are not to charge for something freely given us."

"The gift of salvation, unfortunately man has taken upon himself to have the gall to charge for the Gospel. Paul the Apostle worked with his hands as a tent maker to supply his daily needs. He worked during the day and evenings preached a message of salvation and of repentance. There are exceptions, some of the times he accepted offerings, but whenever he could, he worked so that he was not a burden to anyone. Only by God's grace our congregation, pay's my expenses and furnishes a home free of charge.

I believe that the congregation expects too much from the minister. He can only take his congregation as far as he has done himself." He stood up and said to those who were left in the Restaurant, "it's time for us to go to our respective homes. I want to thank each and every one of you for being here to see the glory of God at work. I also want to thank Gil and of course his wife Sarah, a Godly woman who never lost faith in God's healing virtue. Join me in a closing prayer for what he has done in our midst. We bless your Holy name oh Holy One, and from our hearts we give thanks to You!" Amen!

As soon as all of them left, except Gil and Sarah. Gil had motioned to the Preacher that he wanted to see him in private. "Reverend I have some good news. I received a call from the State AG concerning the reopening of the

Bustamante boy's case. He said that he put enough pressure on the Judge for him to call the Nineth Circuit court of Appeals and he said that after reading the transcript of the trial' he ordered the State to release him Immediately. He said how could a district Judge allow such a railroad trial, of a US citizen. He ordered a new trial to be held in a couple of weeks and that Manny be released Monday morning, he will be home tomorrow evening. He was very angry at the way the county DA handled the case, along with The Coroner and Sheriff Brady."

"Another thing I did Reverend, I filed an application to run for the office of San Lois Obispo County Sheriff. The office of registration is open until noon on Saturdays." "You left me speechless Reverend and blessed what God can do when He wants injustice to be reversed." "What about the weapon Gil?" "They have an Idea who the owner is, the MO is our friend Tony Guardino." "Gil, it sounds like all the pieces of the puzzle are falling into place. There is another individual that I feel is also involved. I need to speak with the AG, do you have a number where I can reach him?" "Write it down, it is a private number. It will be ok, just tell him I told you to call him. He is a very nice man and easy to talk to. Preacher, we need to get going, it's almost six PM. One more thing, can we get together on Monday?" "How about 1:00 PM." "That's fine Gil, see you Monday."

He walked out of the building and thought how a T-bone steak would taste right now. There was a steak house in Cambria, but was not sure if it was open, then he remembered that this state had Blue-Laws. Maybe he could get one from the restaurant, take it home and cook it on the grill. He had a key, but he couldn't find any in the freezer, so he did the next best thing, he would have a can of chili beans and a box of crackers, for his dinner when he got home.

The Preacher walked home, and of course he knew that somebody had been in his house He could see where he had left drawers opened. The sheets on his bed had been pulled back, then hastily tried to smooth them down. He looked in his dresser. He had one drawer in use for his underwear and half a dozen socks and a package of new tee-shirts and a small box of personal belongings, which held a wedding ring, a picture of his wife and children and other photos of people he had befriended, along with some letters he had received from people he had helped. What he was looking for was in the State DA's office.

He searched the bathroom and the small closet which contained a couple of wash cloths, hand towels and bath towels. An extra roll of toilet paper and a bar of soap. He went into the kitchen and found nothing had been disturbed. The living room also had been searched. He felt that the intruder had been scared off because he noticed that the back door had been left open. This was the typical back door porch with a large tub for washing clothes. There was a cabinet above the tub which contained a wash board and a couple of bars of lye soap.

He locked the back door and went into the kitchen and put a pot of coffee on. The can of chili-beans he placed on the stove to heat. When the coffee was done, he poured a cup full and decided to eat the beans in the can along with the crackers. Then he took a couple of bites and decided that he needed some fresh onions cutup, so he found some onions that were starting to grow, but good enough to eat with his beans. He was about to pour another cup of coffee when the doorbell rang.

He called out, "come on in." It was Mr. Swensen. He walked into the kitchen as the Preacher said to him, "what a surprise, would you care for a cup of coffee?" "Yes, that sounds good." "What brings you out so late Swede?" "I went to bed and couldn't sleep. I need to confess to you what a double life I have been leading."

"Let me start from the beginning. Shortly after the government passed the law that it was illegal to make, buy and sell any type of spirits. One day one of the men in our church came to me and told me that he had been approached by the Sheriff and asked if he was interested in allowing him to store whiskey in a small building in the forest, used for storing tools. I asked my friend had he considered, that it was illegal and if caught, the penalty would destroy him and his family.   Since he worked for the state land management, I hesitated and finally said yes. He then asked me if I would be interested in being part of the deal. Our job would be to store and transport the Illegal whiskey, and make sure it was safe. At this point my flesh got the best of me and rationalized that I needed the money. I was about to lose our ranch and home and went along with it. As things got better, I was able to get out of debt and have extra money to give to the church."

"This is only the beginning of the story. One day I was doing the books of the church, when George Cain walked in. With him were Sherriff Martin Grady and the county Coroner. George said, "Swede we have a problem; we found out that someone had discovered one of our storage shed's. We are about to be exposed, if we don't silence the person, who is a young woman. The Big Fellow, from Chicago sent a guy to make sure the girl is silenced, his name is Tony Guardino have you met him Preacher?" The Preacher said, "I have Swede, you don't want to tangle with him. Continue with your story." George said, "we came to warn you if anyone asks about Bootleg Whiskey, if asked, you don't know a thing. If you violate our agreement, you know the ramifications, am I clear? And if we get caught, we all spend time in a Federal Prison." The Sheriff told me to tell you Reverend to stay out of their business, or else? That's all he said."

The Preacher asked Swede, "why didn't you try and get a loan to help pay some of your debt. It sounds like your faith is very week. I hope you realize what your family will go through. You were considered an Elder. You jeopardized the safety of your family, when they find out, how will they react? Those in the community as well. I don't have to tell you how vicious these mobsters are. They can become brutal when somebody crosses them. I want to pray to our heavenly Father that he will protect you because of your willingness to help bring them to justice."

The Preacher said, "the death of the girl was a tragedy. Your reputation will injure others who trusted you, I forgive you and I know our Lord has because you asked for forgiveness. I will ask Gil Snowden to help us, he knows a lot of good lawyers. It's in God that we trust; I have one more question, why didn't you go and tell the authorities?" "I was told that if I went to the authorities, they would kill me and my family. Each time I met with George; he would remind me of their little secret. So, I went along with them, then I stopped taking their money and told them I didn't want their blood money. They sent their muscleman, Guardino, to warn me, if I breathed one word to anyone, I would regret it. Now you know the truth Reverend" The Preacher responded, "Swede, we have someone to help with a solid defense. I suppose you have lived in fear all this time." "Yes Reverend, a day doesn't go by that I ask God for help." The Preacher said, "why do you think I was sent here? I remind you that you need to trust God in everything we encounter in this life."

The Preacher said, "Look, it's getting late, but if it's alright with you, I will call Gil and tell him our plight. I'll call him in the morning. One more thing, I recommend you tell your family. I'll be in touch with you. Have a good night's sleep; before you go, let me pray with you" He prayed for guidance and peace for all the Swensen family. The Preacher started to weep for Swede and his family. He knew he would be forgiven by them."

He wept for the Christians who are subjected to trials in life's journey, that each trial brings them closer to God. Faith and God's grace are the things we depend on for Him to work in our lives. Men like Swede are very vulnerable because of their gifting, always ready to help someone in trouble. They seem to always get burned. He is a good man who made an error in judgment, which became a sin. My prayer for him and his family that his sentence will be a three-year jail term, suspended, because he was coerced and threatened bodily by a group of thugs. The Preacher said, "Swede go home to your family. Before you go give me a big hug." As he escorted him to the door.

The Preacher needed to relax so he decided to take a shower. The hot water felt good on his weary back and body. It soothed him till finally he ran out of hot water, then dried off, put on his night clothes, jumped into bed and within five minutes he was sound asleep.

He awoke early in the morning. Went to the bath room. Shaved and brushed his teeth, then dressed and put a pot of coffee on to brew. He went into the living room with his cup of coffee and sat down to write a letter to the church board and then sealed the letter, which stated. "To be opened after I have departed." He would take the letter and place it in the Pastors study in the safe where money was kept after the Sunday offering. He had two appointments scheduled, one at ten and one at two this afternoon.

Since the restaurant was closed, he decided to go to a coffee house a couple of blocks from the church. The name of the place was Cambria Bar and Grill, open for breakfast. He walked over to an empty table next to a window. He glanced at the clock on the wall, which read 7:20AM. There was a menu on the table that said, breakfast only. He decided to have a stack of flap jacks and two eggs over medium and a cup of coffee.

A man approached his table, a small thin man with a very crocked nose. He had a head of thick black hair streaked with grey. He looked like an ex-boxer. The man came over to his table and said, "You must be new in town, what brings you out so early? He said." "I am new in town I'm the new minister of The Christian Church of Cambria. I generally get up at sunrise, and fix my own breakfast, but I thought I would try your place." The Preacher asked, "are you the cook also?" "No; I own the place. I was smarter than most fighters, I saved most of my money, and paid outright cash for this place. My wife is the cook for breakfast only. We have a chef that cooks' dinner and a young cook who prepares lunches. We are closed only on Sundays not because of the Blue Law but because God says we are to honor the Sabbath. We attend the Orthodox church about ½ mile North of here. We have three kids. See those pictures on the wall of me when I was fighting. I fought as a feather weight, under the name of Bo Polanski. I had 78 fights record of 69 wins and 9 losses. I teach youth boxing in a gym a couple of doors down; three times a week. I do it for nothing, I believe in this Country, since I was born in Poland. We came to America when I was four years old. My father died shortly after we arrived, so we moved in with my uncle who made us work at a very young age. I only went to fifth grade. I have been going to night school so I can become a Citizen. Why am I saying all this to you,

I'm sorry, let me take your order?"

The Preacher was smiling all the time Bo was talking. "I want an order of Flap Jacks two eggs over medium and a cup of coffee." The Preacher liked him right away, he knew that he was a man of integrity. He prayed for Bo and asked the Lord to bless his wife and his children. He was praying softly when Bo returned with a huge stack of Flap Jacks.

"Reverend, do you want maple syrup or honey?" "Mr. Polanski you can bring me both, since I like both of them." "No problem, Reverend." "Mr. Polanski would you care to join me for breakfast?" "No, thank you, I had breakfast earlier, but if you don't mind, I will have a cup of coffee with you." "Good sit down, Mr. Polanski," "please Padre, call me Bo, I only use my Sir name when I am introducing my wife and mother." "Ok, Bo. can I ask you a question?" "Of course, I have nothing to hide Sir" as he started coughing and stopped when he had to take medicine." The Preacher asked Bo; "how long have you had that cough." "I have what we call black lung disease Padre. When I was a boy, I had to work in the Pennsylvania coal mines. Most men who work in the mines contact this illness, there is no cure for it, so I will die young. Padre I am only 38 years old." As he started to cough again. The next thing that happened the Preacher reached over and touched Bo, and said, "Lord of the universe heal this servant of yours oh merciful Father in the name of our Lord and Savior Christ Jesus" All of a sudden Bo stopped coughing, and started breathing normal."

"What did you do to me Padre?" "I didn't do anything, the Lord healed you, you will live to a ripe old age. Give Him Praise and Glory" "Bo was crying tears of Joy, when his wife came out from the kitchen to see what was going on. "Bo cried out, thank you Lord for my healing, as he shouted to his wife, Tasha my love, as she ran over and said, what is this all about?" "The man sitting their prayed for me. He is the new minister of Cambria Christian Church. Padre this is my wife, Tasha." She was a large rotund woman with jet black hair and deep blue eyes, with a twinkle on her face when she smiled. "My Bo love of my life I am full of joy of our Lord Jesus Christ. Reverend it is my pleasure to know you, may I ask you what your name is?" "My name is Leonardo Flynn, and it is a pleasure to know you both, By the way your Flap Jacks are one of the best I have ever eaten."

"Tasha said, it is an honor to meet a true man of God, if you please excuse me, I must return to the kitchen, because the morning crowd will be arriving. In fact, here comes a few. Please come back soon." She then returned to the kitchen. Two waitresses came walking in for the early crowd. Bo was still sitting in a euphoric state. He reached over and shook the Preachers hand and began to weep softly, then composed himself when the Preacher softly said, "when you go to Mass this Sunday lite a candle for me. I know your heart, along with your wife. You are a blessing to many others. You have felt the power of God, when He is exalted. I must leave due to some church commitments. I hope to come back soon. You will always be in my heart. God bless you both." The Preacher left to go back to his home. He wept a few tears along the way, as he continued to thank God for healing a righteous man.

As he opened the door, he knew that there was someone in the house as he walked into the kitchen, he recognized who was sitting at his table, Sheriff Martin Grady. The Preacher said to him, "who gave you the right to come into my home without my permission. I don't remember inviting you, Sir you have used your office and violated the very oath that you swore to uphold. Why have you broken into my home?" "Look Preacher, I have tried to keep you out of my business. I sent you a warning when we took your little dog from you, I am prepared to go further, this is my last warning. If you value your life you will listen to what I am saying to you" "Excuse me Sheriff, are you threatening me?" "Take it for what it's worth, next time we meet you will see."

The Preacher said, "I have one question, when did

you sell your soul to the devil, he will come soon and will send you to hell. The day you went astray was when you saw your wife with another man. Your anger was intensified when she found out the things you were getting into. Your rage almost killed her, but you used your office to cover up the beatings, lying that an intruder broke into your home. You said you found her in a coma to cover up your sin. There is only one problem, God new what you did, and Satan can't cover it up for you. This is one of the reasons I am here in Cambria."

"I have spoken with the State Attorney General's office and they have issued a warrant for your arrest. Which has long been coming." The Sheriff turned around and faced the Preacher with a look of rage, as he yelled profanities and saying, "I'm going to kill you, Holy man, like right now." He started to charge the Preacher, but stopped and couldn't move, frozen in his tracks. The Preacher looked around for something to tie him up, so he could call the State Police. He walked outside to the clothes line and pulled it down and went back inside and tied his arms and wrist, then drug him to the floor and hog tied him. Then went to the Restaurant called the State Police, He told them that they needed a stenographer to take a deposition. When he finished the call, he went back to the house to wait for the authorities to arrive.

The Preacher heard the knock on the door and said, "come on in." He looked at the clock and saw that it was 10 AM when in walked Deborah and Kyle, "oh my, I thought about you walking in. I thought I had enough time, when I walked into the house and found our illustrious Sheriff sitting at my kitchen table. He threatened to kill me. Somehow, I was able to overcome his charge at me, I tied him up. I'm waiting for the State Police to arrest and book Mr. Brady for Murder, Bootlegging, money laundering and his attempt to kill me. I have proof of all the accusations. I'm sorry that you came on time, I have no way of contacting others, I highly suggest that the church install a telephone in the parsonage."

"Reverend we came to tell you that we received a call from the Army hospital, they want us to come to San Francisco Veterans hospital. We will be gone the rest of the week. Perhaps we can reschedule when we return, if that's all right with you?" "Have a good trip, and of course we can meet when you return. Let me pray for you for safety and a good report from the doctors." After he prayed, he saw them to their car as they left. *He thought of, (Roman 8:28 KJV) And we know that all things work together for good to them that love God, to them who are the called according to his purpose."* Thank You Father for answering my prayers. They will be fine, as your Word say's.

He walked back into the house and waited another half hour, when a State Trooper knocked on the door, the Preacher opened the door and standing with him were two other men. One was the Trooper and a State Recorder. He was surprised that the State District Attorney was with them. "May we come in, ah, Reverend." "My name is Lorenzo Flynn, please come in, and follow me into the kitchen. I'm sure you know this man, the Sheriff of San Luis Obispo, Martin Brady." "Reverend why did you Hog tie him?" "Mr. Clark, he threatened me after I told him of his sins, the next thing I know he lunged at me, after I warned him, that God would strike him dead, if he didn't repent of his sins. He still kept charging me, when he stopped dead in his tracks, frozen."

"I went outside, cut the clothes line and while he was in this trance, I then tied him up." The State AG said, "Sounds like a ferry-tale to me, wait a minute are you the man they call the Preacher?" "Yes I am." "I read about you in the papers a few weeks ago that you risked your life to save four fishermen, every one said it was one of the most heroic acts they had ever seen." The Preacher said, "I have always been a strong swimmer, but my Lord Jesus Christ gave me the strength. I saw human beings in trouble, so I reacted and dove into the water. I'm sure others would have done the same. As to the matter of the Sheriff, the only thing I can think of, God intervened supernaturally."

"I made a Citizen's arrest, just before he made his threats. The rest of the charges are documented by one of the men on our Deacon Board. Swede Swensen, he lives a couple of blocks from here. He will verify the man's involvement in the mob, and the threats he made against Mr. Swensen. Mr. Swensen will also need a good attorney, since he is partially guilty for knowing about the bootleggers using Cambria as a drop off point, and knowledge of the girl that was killed.

I almost forgot, agent Gil Snowden our friend wanted to see where the body of the girl was found and where I found the knife. We walked into the woods where my little dog found the girls remains. Another day while walking in the same area I saw a glimmer shining a few feet where she had lain. I went over and dug close to the object until it was totally uncovered and saw that it was a special kind of knife, Gil said it was a Stiletto. I then wrapped it in a handkerchief, in case there were prints on the knife. Gil took it and said he would give it to you. The DA said, "Reverend, I personally want to thank you for being a good citizen. I wish there were more like you." "You are too kind Sir."

The DA said, "I know of only one individual in the

Mob that uses such a weapon, Tony Guardino. Has he been seen in these parts?" "I met him here in Cambria the same day the boat blew up. He came over to me and asked me if I had seen any bottles that had not exploded. He also said the he was a Federal Agent assigned to this area. When I asked him for his ID, he said that he had left it in the hotel. He sure is a creepy individual. That's all I know, if there is any more, I don't remember." The DA said, "thanks for being so open minded, where did you say that Swede Swensen lives?" "You go one block East, turn left on the first block going North. Continue a few houses, until you see on your right a Victorian home sign that says, The Swensen's Welcome." "Okay Reverend, hope to see you again in the future." As they drove off, "perhaps, said the Preacher."

CHAPTER 16

Two weeks passed after the arrest of the Sheriff and his cohorts. They were charged with various felonies pertaining to murder, money laundering and bootlegging. Swede Swensen was charged for his participation with bootlegging, he is on bail and will testify for the State. Manuelo Bustamante was released from prison and cleared from all charges. The County DA is also under indictment for trial maleficence. He has been stripped of his lawyer's license and disbarred from office immediately.

The congregation, at first was shocked, especially about two deacons who were involved with the Mob. The head Deacon was involved as one of the leaders. His death is under investigation. The church would select two new deacons, to fill the loss of Deacon Cain and Swede.

The Preacher presented a sermon on forgiveness His "I stand here today to speak to you about those who abuse power. King David was the king of Israel who abused his power to cover up his adultery, with Bathsheba, then had her husband killed to cover up his indiscretion. He was forgiven by God when he repented. It took Nathan the prophet to expose King David. King David was not a very good father as you can see by the actions of a couple of his sons, one raped his sister and later killed by Absalom because his father did nothing to reprimand his brother Amnon. Absalom later tried to take the Kingdom away from King David. He later died at the hands of some of David's men. He then spoke of the betrayal of Peter against the Lord, when he denied Him. Jesus forgave him after he had risen. Forgiveness is an act of the will." He went on to say, "that if the Lord forgives you, please don't hesitate to forgive those who sin against you. Those who repent are forgiven because He loves us."

The following day, the Preacher was sitting at his kitchen table drinking a cup of coffee after he had showered. He was waiting for a sweet roll to warm, when he heard a knock at the door. He jumped up and went to the door and was taken back by a young couple. The young man spoke up, "are you Rev. Lorenzo Flynn?" "Yes, I am, and whom am I speaking to?" "I am Peter Jeremiah and my wife Lydia. Our little girl is Sarah; she is four years old." "Please come into the house. Have you had breakfast yet?" "No sir, we have been traveling for four days, eating Baloney and Penult Butter sandwiches.' Last night we slept in a camp. All we had was a cup of coffee this morning."

"Come follow me to the Cambria restaurant. We will go for breakfast, today is Tuesday and Mrs. Bustamante, is cooking this morning. She started doing the cooking last week. She cooks American and Mexican."

They walked in, just as Deborah came out of the kitchen. She rushed over to them and placed them at a brand-new table. As she said, "we are in the process of renovating the restaurant. We have added a Mexican Menu as well. We just received our new tables and the remodeling is going on in the large room first, then in here. I'm so excited about it. "Reverend, would you please introduce your friends." "Forgive me said the Preacher, they just got here from Texas and we have a very hungry little girl. Her name is Sarah, her mother and father Lydia and Peter Jeremiah. They too are hungry, put the tab on my account Deborah if you don't mind." Deborah said, "glad to know all of you, now what can I serve you?" Sarah said, "I want flapjacks and chocolate milk." Lydia and Peter said, "we both would like Eggs Rancheros with beans on the side and coffee with flour tortillas." Deborah said, "Coming right up, how about juice, some freshly squeezed Oranges? Bring me a large glass, what about both of you, Peter and Lydia?" Peter said, we're fine miss."

Deborah took the order with her and soon returned with a plate of hot steaming flapjacks and a large glass of chocolate milk. She set the dish in front of Sarah, then went back to the kitchen and waited a few minutes while Angelina prepared the Mexican breakfast. When she finished, Angelina Bustamante helped with the servings. Deborah said, "This is Angelina Bustamante who cooked the Mexican food, this is her fifth day on the job. The Preacher said, "Deborah why don't you join us for at least a cup of coffee?" "Yes, I will until the morning crowd starts coming."

They were all trying to talk while eating their meal. Deborah went to the kitchen and in a few minutes returned with a stack of flapjacks, and said, "I couldn't help smelling the pancakes, as people from the South call them flapjacks. They are scrumptious." As she took another bite and a big gulp of coffee.

The Preacher spoke up and said, "how do you like the Mexican food, you won't find any better. As a Texan having worked in the fields with the campesinos' for two years, I learned to eat tacos and tortas, along with burritos. Sometimes they were filled with beans chicken and rice, or Chile Verde or Colorado, spiced then topped off with Cilantro for flavor. I loved the food along with the people. I miss the time I spent with them working in the fields, until I came here. I have been here almost two months and have come to love the people in the church. I am Irish and Spanish my mother was Spanish and taught me the language. Just a short synopsis on how I came to Cambria. Peter why don't you tell us about yourself?"

"I suppose my narrow road journey in the Rio Grande valley as a boy. My Father was a Baptist Preacher of a small town where we lived. He was a very kind man and trusted everyone. One night during prayer meeting a fellow came in who had been drinking. He hadn't been in the church for more than a couple of minutes when he stood up and started screaming profanities at my Dad; calling him a hypocrite. Accusing him of having an affair with his wife. She was being counseled by my father. She was in the church and went over to her husband, about the same time he pulled a revolver and aimed it at her, Dad tried to wrestle the gun from him when it went off, killing my father. The man ran out of the church and was never seen again. I was twelve years old when this happened. I was the oldest son of five children. I always wanted to be like my father. He never refused a person in need. He always said to trust the Lord always. He would get extra work or someone would send him a small amount of money to help our family. He would worship and pray to the Lord every-day. Sometimes he would fast when it was a major problem. I never heard him say an unkind word about anyone. He adored my mother. He loved all of us kids. He would always encourage me to study God's word and meditate on scriptures, that would become part of my soul. I had to go to work part time working for a Godly neighbor. Dad always said when you run into a problem that you can't resolve, take it to the Lord in prayer."

"When I finished grade school I applied for a special grant and received a four-year grant to go to seminary. I am working on a master of divinity at present. I didn't have to go into the military because of being the eldest child and needed to help the family."

"I met my wife Lydia at a church social. We started dating and after six months of courtship, her father and mother approved of the marriage. Our first pastorate was in a small town close to Midland Texas, it was a learning process to say the least. The town dried up due to the only manufacturing company closing, so most of the people left and found work elsewhere."

"We have been praying for guidance and a new church opening. One day while praying God said to us to go West to California, so we took off. I felt like Abraham, when God called him to the Land of Canaan. Abraham obeyed God and set out to the promised land. As we got closer to California while camping, I took out a map of California and started looking at all the small communities, when my eye saw the town of Paso Robles. I thought it was the place he had been directing me too. We arrived in Paso Robles yesterday and camped in a state park near the town. Lydia and I were discussing, weather to stay in Paso Robles and see the town in the morning, or get up early and drive here to the coast. We both prayed and looked at the map again and saw the name Cambria. We both heard God clearly say, Cambria. So here we are, but I find that you already have a minister."

As his face saddened, he almost had tears in his eyes, when the Preacher said to Deborah, "would you please excuse us for a few minutes, I need to comfort our brother and sister, thank you." As she made her way to the kitchen. The Preacher told them why he came to Cambria and what he found when he arrived. It was a special assignment to help put the pieces back together of the congregation and establish a new deacon board.

He told them how corrupt the church had become because of greed and a lust for power by those in authority. He said, "that God told him to set things in order. Paul the Apostle sent Timothy to Corinth to correct immoral behavior. You will be God's Timothy for Cambria. As to how long I will be here, most likely no more than no two weeks, please keep this to yourself. I knew you were on your way from Texas and have been expecting you."

"We need to get you into the Parsonage. I will sleep on the couch until I leave, if that's alright with you both. The woman's group remodeled and painted, the entire interior and replaced all the drapes and curtains in all the windows. The ice box needs to be replaced by one of the new refrigerators, tonight is the deacon board meeting. I will check and see if they can buy a new one and install a telephone. There is a cellar, which I have never been in. When we get back to the Parsonage, we can check it out." Deborah came back to the table when she saw the Preacher get up to leave. The Preacher took his wallet out and gave Deborah a Ten Dollar bill and said, "this should cover the bill." Deborah said, "put your money away, it's no good in here." The Preacher said, "God bless your generosity, Deborah. From now on your business will prosper for years to come. You will see your grandchildren to the fourth generation, said the Lord. I understand Kyle is working the farm, he too will prosper for many years, and your sons will serve this country in the military in the distant future." He said a prayer for Kyle and Deborah and their two sons. They returned to the parsonage and went into the house.

Lydia placed Sarah down for her nap. Gil Snowden showed up. The Preacher introduced him to Peter and Lydia. The Preacher along with Peter and Gil went outside. The Preacher said, "I want to check out the Cellar, would you gentlemen join me." Gil and Peter said, both agreed. There was a lock on the Cellar door and the Preacher did not have a key, but remembered there was a key ring with three keys hanging near the door jam. He returned to the Cellar entrance. He found a key he felt was the one, he was correct for the lock. He put the key in the lock as it slipped off very easy. It had been used a lot. The Preacher lifted the door, found a light switch and made his way down the stairs. It was larger than he had thought. There was the usual shelfing, with home-made soups, canned peaches, apricots and all sorts of canned Jelly's, there were several cans of bully beef, recently purchased.

On one side was a huge tarp covering some boxes that had been tied with a large amount of rope. The Preacher asked Peter to help him remove the tarps from the boxes. When they finally had taken the tarps off, all they could say was wow. After they had finished counting the boxes of Scotch Whiskey. Worth a small fortune on the bootleg booze market. There were also a few cases of very expensive wine. They had no clue as to how much money was involved. The Preacher said, to Gil, "what do you think the agency will say about your find?" Gil said, "I don't know other than good work agent Snowden, probably an Atta boy. I will call a couple of agents and tell them of our find. They will know how much it's worth. They live in

San Luis Obispo less than two hours away. I will call them to bring a truck. Let's place the tarps back on the cases, then I'll make the call.

They went back upstairs as Gil Snowden walked over a block away and found a shop who had a phone. The phone rang only a couple of times when a familiar voice of a fellow agent answered "This is agent Herman speaking." "Harry this is Snowden I need you and Bert to come to Cambria. You won't believe what we found at the Preachers home a block from the restaurant. We discovered over a hundred cases of the finest Scotch alcohol and a few cases of imported wine, mostly collector's vintage. You better bring a small truck so that you can transport the Alcohol to wherever you dispose of confiscated alcohol. I'm sorry I had to bother you." "GIL, did you register for the Sheriff election?" "Yes, I did Harry, why do you ask?" "I will fill you in when you get here, but the State Attorney was here and they arrested him, handcuffs and all to book him, in other words the law caught up to the scoundrel. As I said I'll tell you all about it when you get here." "Before I forget Gil, how is your wife?" "She is so beautiful and so humble. Her Family is thinking of visiting our church this Sunday, they rarely go to church and have never made a commitment to our Lord, we shall see. See you in a couple of hours. Bye."

He went back to the Parsonage as the Preacher was singing, "What a Mighty God we Serve." He heard a female voice that sounded like an operatic voice, it was voice of Lydia, wife of the young minister. The Preacher stopped when he heard her voice, it was as an Angel was singing from Heaven. She continued singing until she finished the song. The Preacher and Gil were standing with tears of Joy as she completed the song. They were so entranced with her voice they couldn't find words to compliment her. Finely the Preacher asked her, "have you had professional training?" She Replied, "when I was a young girl about nine, I asked the Lord to bless me with the gift of singing. I was always shy about my voice, until that day when I gave my heart to Him. I promised Him that I would only sing at Christian Churches or gatherings." The Preacher said, "in all my life on this earth I have never heard a voice as wonderful as yours. Would you sing a solo this Sunday?" Lydia responded, "It would be an honor Reverend." "Good, it will bless all the people, and Honor Our Lord!" The preacher said he felt he needed to be alone for a breather. Gil waited in the back yard for his fellow agents with the truck to transport the alcohol.

The Preacher thought to himself what a blessed morning, that was quickly approaching lunch time. He loved the smell of the Ocean, even from here he could feel a gentle breeze and a salty smell that at times would clear your sinus. He thought that if he was raising a family, the area was ideal for raising children. A few miles up the coast was San Semeion the home of the Newspaper Tycoon Randolph Hearst. Many of the famous Movie Stars drove through Cambria to visit and stay with the big man. He has a huge menagerie of wild exotic animals. Further up the coast you will be treated to one of God's creation, Elephant Seals as they come onto shore by the thousands to birth their calf's. He was lost in his thoughts and humming a Christian song, *"How Great Thou Art"*.

The next thing you know he is at his front door and didn't realize he had walked so far. As he walked in Sarah and Lydia were studying the Bible and Peter was unloading his car and small trailer, full of all their personal belongings. They were startled when He opened the door and walked in. He saw Peter struggling with the load of clothing he held in his arms, as the Preacher said, "let me clear out my meager clothing and for now I will use the front closet in the living room and store my stuff in there, if that's ok with you?" "Sir this is still your home and we are the intruders." "No such thing, you are my guests until I am no longer the minister of this congregation." He quickly unloaded all his stuff and put them in his travel bag and the other clothes he hung in the closet, which were two shirts another suit and a set of denim trouser and an old pull over sweater.

His shaving gear would stay in the bathroom. It took about an hour to put away all their belongings. I will call Gil so he can eat with us. He went outside and asked Gil in for a late lunch. Lydia said, "I think it's time for a break, what if I make a batch of Tuna Fish Sandwiches, there is milk in the ice box and onions, but no celery but plenty of bread and a couple of apples and a can of peaches." As they all started laughing, because of the canned fruit in the cellar. Lydia said, "you three gentlemen go into the living room, I will call you when lunch is ready."

"Lunch is ready gentlemen." she had set her good China on the table that had belonged to her grandmother. The Preacher and Peter along with Gil ate two sandwiches apiece and a half of an apple and a couple of peaches. The young minister ate his sandwiches with a large glass of iced tea. About the time that they finished lunch, the two agents Harry and Bert with two other agents and a large truck that belonged to the agency. It took them about an hour and a half to load all the cases of alcohol. The Preacher motioned to Gil that he wanted to speak to him in private, so they went outside for a walk. The Preacher told Peter and Lydia that Gil and He had a few things to discuss that were private.

They decided to walk into the woods since fall was

in the air and still warm. Gil spoke up first, "Reverend what was so important that you needed to speak to me in private, and what about?" "I struggle to share with you about my role here in Cambria. I will be leaving in a couple of weeks, because I am needed somewhere else. I have come to truly love all of you, but my ministry is very limited. I don't stay very long in one place. I knew this when I came here. I have never had any real close friends, you come the closest to one in many years. I plan to leave two Sundays from now after services, but I ask that what I tell you, do not tell a soul, nor under any circumstance say anything about our conversation." "Reverend, I look to you as a big brother and will treasure our meeting and caring for each other as true brothers." The Preacher said, "Thanks, to you, you will always have a special place in my heart for you and your family. The other thing is what and how I was involved with the arrest of the Sheriff. Let's find a nice big rock and sit."

They found what they were looking for and sat down on the place close to where the girl's body was found. They sat there for about half an hour while the Preacher told Gil how he set a trap for the killer knowing that he would trap himself due to his greedy human nature. The Preacher said, "we need to get back to the house and see how your men are doing with the contraband. By the way; where and what do you do with the alcohol that is confiscated." Gil said, "In this particular case, we contact the Canadian Government to see if this was stolen, or sold. If stolen we ask them where and ask them if they want us to dispose of it, or if they wish to come and pick it up? It depends on the price verses the cost of shipping it back. Since this is very expensive alcohol, most likely they will come and pick it up." "Let's get going, said the Preacher."

It took them about fifteen minutes to get back to the house. About the time Agents were just loading the last couple of cases. The other two agents had left and went home. Hauling bottles can be a very delicate job, making sure the bottles are secure in the straw packing. Then they had a special strapping to secure each case. Gil said, "good job gentlemen, are you planning on taken the load to Canada?" "The Canadian Government is paying a good price. Harry said, "that he called the Canadian Government. They said they would pay us for delivering the alcohol. It wouldn't make much difference if we loaded them on a freight train, clear up to Vancouver, the drive can be brutal."

Harry said, I called the Boss and he gave us permission, to drive and paid our expenses, plus a two-week vacation. Were both going, Maybe, do a bit of fishing, I understand they have streams that the fish ask you, please take me." They all started to laugh, Gil said, "I have heard some big fish tales, but I think you will be begging the fish to bite your hook. If The fish don't bite. Any way, if you guys are leaving from here don't try and go on highway 1, drive back to Paso, go North on highway 101and about three to four days from now you will reach the border of Canada. Please be careful. Be on the lookout for robbers and Highjack gangs."

They had camping gear and food supplies so the trip was also a small vacation. The Preacher thought to himself he would love to have been going along, but God comes first in all things. The years he spent working with the itinerant workers. The name in Spanish Campesino's, means campers. The Preacher noticed that Harry and Burt were ready to get going.

The Preacher said, "Gentlemen let me pray that God will give you a safe journey there and back. 'Heavenly Father we pray for these two men for a safe journey, and that they return safe to their families, I ask that they would be a blessing for all those they come in contact with. we Give You Praise, Honor and Glory that you richly deserve.' Amen!" They all said, "so be it."

CHAPTER 17

The Preacher glanced at the clock and saw that it was 4 PM. He knew he had a Board meeting; the main agenda, who to replace the two members who were no longer Deacons. Under the circumstances that led to this special meeting. Replacement for Swede's position, would be hard to fill.

He had been praying for guidance, and to know the hearts of the other Deacons. He was anxious to hear what they had to say. He was thinking what he would say, when Gil said, 'Preacher I have to hit the road, it's getting late. I have a backlog of paper work, open and closed cases. Then mail a report to Washington D.C." He said goodbye then drove off going South to return to San Luis Obispo, a difficult journey due to the rocky narrow road.

The Preacher loved Gil, like Jonathan loved David. *He remembered his younger brother who succumbed; to the ravages of diphtheria long ago, there were times he thought about Erick how he would want the Preacher to rock him to sleep. There was a fourteen-year difference in age, but he died at four years of age. Tears welled up and he soon found himself crying.*

He was interrupted by a knock at the door, it was Deborah and Kyle. The Preacher said, "what a pleasant surprise, come on in." Peter said, if this is a private matter, Lydia and I can go outside it's still a nice day." The Preacher said, "it is, but we can sit in that old bench in back, if that's ok with you?" Kyle and Deborah said, "yes sir, it would be much better between the three of us." "Do either of you want a cup of coffee?" "Yes, that would be fine, besides we can take it with us in those large cups."

They walked to the back of a long yard where at the end was an old redwood bench, that had been painted several times. Kyle and Deborah sat on the bench, while the Preacher sat in front on the soft green grass. He said, "what's going on between you two?" "Kyle responded; "we are having a hard time in our love making. Something always seems to interrupt us. I think I'm the one who has the problem, sometimes I think that God is repaying me for the things I did in the war, I don't know, I am so confused." "Oh honey, you haven't given us enough time together, you are still wounded in your heart." "The Preacher said, "what I'm about to ask you is very personal, but you must be truthful with the Lord. Have either of you had sexual relations with anyone else during your ten-year separation, be sure you are truthful." Deborah, started crying and, "asked Kyle to forgive her. She said after seven years when they declared you dead, I started dating a man in the church and soon we were talking marriage, so one night in a moment of passion, I lost control and slept with him. A few weeks passed and he was gone; it turns out the man was married and was separated from his wife, but they decided to try to mend their differences. I take an oath that it was the only time, I had relations with another man. I ask God to forgive me in front of you, my husband."

The Preacher said, "how about you Kyle, did you commit adultery when you were in France?" He hesitated and said, "yes, "when I was on a weekend leave with a couple of buddies, we went to this beer joint to have a couple of beers, the waitress was a young French girl. I spent the night with her, after this we went back to the front. You know the rest of the story, I had memory loss, but only by the grace of God I am home. I too bare responsibility for my actions, there is no excuse, I sinned against God and you my dear, can you forgive me?" "Oh Kyle, I do with all my heart, if you will still want me." Kyle got up and went over and hugged her as they both wept in each other's arms."

The Preacher waited until they composed themselves, then he said, "when you got back from being lost for almost ten years, both of you never trusted God to forgive you of your sins, because neither one of you confessed to God for forgiveness. Both of you have carried this guilt long enough. As God forgave David and I'm sure He forgave Bathsheba. Both of you feel guilty each time you try to make love. Today you have been set free. There is one more thing I, want you to do, rededicate your marriage vows to the Lord Jesus Christ."

"I want both of you to get up and kneel before me and repeat these words. Do you Kyle take this woman to be your wife, in sickness and in health till death do you part, say I do. Do you Deborah take Kyle as your lawful wedded husband to honor and respect him through sickness and in health till death. Say I do." Both of them said we do. I pronounce you man and wife. Today you have entered a covenant marriage with each other and it is sanctified by the Lord. Amen! You may kiss your wife." As they both hugged and kissed each other.

"One more thing that will last a life time. Ecclesiastes states that a three stranded rope is not easily broken, one strand will hold the other two, it being Christ. Rope makers will tell you that the strongest rope made is a three stranded one, like the Holy Trinity cannot be broken. There is a saying, they tied the knot. Go with my blessings, and remember if you have a problem seek, God's advice in His word. Now go home, oh I almost forgot there is a Deacon meeting at the church in the Pastor's study. Kyle you are invited."

The Preacher went back into the house and decided to take a shower. Peter and Lydia were in the living room playing with Sarah. He went into the living room and said that he would be using the bathroom for a while. He said, "would you like to join me for dinner at the restaurant. You can order American or Mexican, think it over until I get through showering, sound ok to you?" "Yes sir, it would be our pleasure." "It's all set we eat first then I go to the church at seven, Peter if you wish to join me you are welcome." "It would be an honor Reverend." The Preacher said, "It's set then, I better hurry it's getting late"

They went to the Restaurant and enjoyed a good meal. After dinner they walked back to the Parsonage, Lydia stayed with Sarah. It took a few minutes to walk to the church. The other deacons were standing outside the church waiting for the Preacher. He said, "good evening, Gentlemen, I hope you are all in good health this evening?" They looked at him, then in unison they all said, "we are fine, then they all laughed. The Preacher said "Please take a seat, so we can get to our main reason, to select two new Deacons replacing two brothers on the board. Since we do not have a head Deacon to chair the meeting, I will chair this special meeting. I hope it meets with your approval." They went around the table and all agreed he was acceptable as temporary chair.

The meeting came to order after they had prayed for guidance and unity in the church. The Preacher introduced Kyle, since most of them joined the church after the war. There was one exception Dan Cartwright, who was the eldest serving Deacon. I invited Kyle to share how our brother Swede is dealing with awaiting trial. Kyle, the floor is yours."

"I am here as a surrogate for my father-in-law. He is so ashamed of being involved with George Cain, because it destroyed his reputation in the church and community. It is a sordid story and no excuse is acceptable. He asked me to tell you all how sorry he was and is waiting on the courts to bring him to trial. His wife and Deborah my wife all feel as I do, but by the grace of God as a family and as Christians we await the outcome. We know that the Lord is merciful and if he has to spend time in prison, he is resolved to comply with any decision the court makes. For myself, I love Swede like my own Father and will make sure his wife is well cared for. Thank you for allowing me to speak for Swede. God bless the members of the congregation and its leadership, I am honored to be part of this church, thank you." There were no questions by any of the Deacons.

The Preacher said, "I would like to make a comment, in behalf of Swede and others who have crossed the line, from light to darkness. God is a God of forgiveness love and acceptance. When we sin and do not repent, God cannot go against His word. These three virtues should be posted on the entrance to the church. I would like all of us to send Swede a letter stating our position. I am reminded of a few words that Christ spoke in (John 8:7KJV). "He who is without sin among you, let him cast the first stone! "We must, in our darkest moments, overcome the adversity with the help from Our Omnipotent God. When we forgive those who spitefully use others, we must always leave the door of forgiveness open. Amen!"

The rest of the meeting dealt with the church finances, maintenance of the church, as well as the parsonage. The Preacher said that they needed a phone in the parsonage, which was approved. He also said that, "it would be nice if they could add another bed room. As to the cost, we have the finances to construct a thirty by forty room with an extra bath room." "Excuse us Reverend, but where are we going to get enough money for such a construction?" "I thought you would never ask. It so happens that this morning, I received a check from the Federal Government for five thousand dollars as a reward for arresting the three men involved, the County Coroner, the Sheriff and our former brother deacon, also Guardino is still wanted for murder."

"I give it to the church as part of a new designated building fund. If anyone of you is in the construction business, please speak up." Gus Albright, spoke up and said, "Reverend I will provide the lumber." "Gary Elder, said, I am a plumber and will provide at cost all materials and I will give the labor free. The rest of the room, roofing and windows and hardware will cost less than we have, so we can furnish the room, also there are two brothers in the church who are carpenters and roofers. I will get them to draw up the plans." Gus said, "I will get the permits, a state inspector is a friend of mine, and besides he is a Christian." "Thank you, gentlemen for working in unity, I'm proud of all of you. One more thing, I want to pray that the Holy Spirit will guide you to the men He wants to replace our former deacons.. We do not need to rush into making a quick decision. If there is no more to discus, let us close in prayer."

The Preacher was very optimistic on the condition of the church. He had two more Sundays, then he would be gone. He walked along with Peter both engrossed in their thoughts. When they got to the Parsonage, the Preacher said to Peter that he was going to walk on for a-while. Peter went into the house as the Preacher kept walking. He didn't realize how far he had walked until he heard the sound of the Sea crashing onto the rocks with a steady beat. The night was very clear because it was a full Moon. When he got to the sea shore, he took off his shoes and walked into the water. He was taken back as he felt a presence he hadn't felt in many years. It was one of the leading angels. He stopped and said, "Lord what do I owe this visit too." "We want to take you now, what do you think?" "I would like to stay two more Sundays if it is allowable? I have a couple of things I want to clean up." "We will extend it through to this Sunday that is all. The Lord told me to tell you what a wonderful ministry you accomplished in Cambria, Love from our Savior."

He was brought back to his senses and his encounter with the Angel of God. He sat back on the sand and lost all track of time. *He thought of his early life in Mexico. His thoughts took him to the small community a few miles from Mexico City. He could smell the cooking of his mother as she made his favorite paella with fish, rice chicken and other ingredients. With fresh sweet breads and rich hot chocolate. His father would sometimes allow him to have a small glass of wine made from their small vineyard. He could still smell the antipasto served with their Sunday meal. He thought of His two sisters and one younger brother. He remembered the day that his brother was killed by a wagon. His Parents, went every Saturday to sell Wine, Grapes Pomegranates,*

Figs and Raisins in the town open market. He wept for a few minutes as he thought of the effects the death of his brother had on his family. He could not recall what his wife and two boys looked like, as if God had wiped his memory of their existence.

He thought about the day he gave his heart to God. He was helping his father prune the grape vines. His father went to their home for some tools. He was humming a Christian tune, when all of a sudden, a bright light shown all around him, as he heard a voice say, Leonardo, you will serve me in many ways, but not in this country, God has a special plan for your life. There is a monastic group that lives in the mountains east of here. I want you to go and visit them. Their Leader will welcome you and tell you what you are to do to prepare you for ministry, you will learn what a true servant is.

He was wakened back to reality by the crashing of the Sea as it pounded the protruding rocks. He looked around and realized he had slept all night on the sand. He felt empty because he remembered the dream about his family and the loss of his wife and children. After his encounter with the Lord, he told his parents that he had to go to the top of the mountain. He was fifteen years old when he went to the monastery. It was a Charismatic Brotherhood who believe that the gifts of the Spirit are for today's church.

He stayed with them for four years. He finished his schooling with the monks. He remembered how fast the time went by. He was to live with them until his nineteenth birthday. He had memorized the New Testament and several books of the Old Testament. When he finished his studies at the monastery, he was prepared to do the Lord's work. He also had to prepare a testimony about his father and mother. His father was Irish and his mother was of Spanish blood, who was born in Mexico

His first assignment was in a remote village in Ecuador working with indigent Indians. He stopped and said to Himself, "Leonardo, stop living in the past. Live for the Lord in His time."

He made his way back to the main part of town and saw that the restaurant lights were on and knocked on the door. Angelina came and opened the door. She said, "Reverend what are you doing out so early, here let me get you a cup of Mexican coffee with canella. Would you like some breakfast?" "Yes, would you please fix me a surprise." "Senior, I will make you my specialty, Huevos Frito's and Chile Verde with papas Frito's con frijoles with queso, and some flour tortillas." She soon came back with a steaming cup of coffee, with a smell he remembered as a boy, a Spanish spice, along with the delicious plate, her specialty. The Preacher asked her to join him for a cup of coffee, she said, "Reverend I have a lot to do before the first customers come, but I can take a few minutes." As she sat down.

He said, "Angelina how is your son adapting to being back home?" "He is doing fine, and is continuing his studies, along with helping his father farm our own land and has his own room. He was offered a scholarship from Stanford University when they heard what had happened to him. He will start school in the fall. Manuelo is so proud of his son and said to me that he still feels sorry for Senior Swensen and his wife. They came to see him and apologized to him for not speaking up sooner. Manuelito is such a forgiving young man, he will be here in about an hour to help in the kitchen for this morning, maybe you will see him. He has said that he wanted to thank you for all that you did for him. Papa, is plowing up the field with a tractor that Senior Swede loaned him. God is such a loving and forgiving Lord. I personally want to thank you as well may He continue to bless you."

"Angelina, you are far to kind to me. We are close to the same age, but you remind me of my mother, always doing for others, it has been a blessing to know you and your husband." She said, "I must go back to work do you want some more coffee?" "Oh yes, it is fantastic." She quickly went to the kitchen and brought back another cup.

His mind wandered back to what he had to do in a couple of days, He always felt empty inside when he had to leave people he had come to admire and love. He thought about having to travel the narrow road again. He was interrupted by a familiar voice. "Good morning, Preacher, how are you this morning, As Deborah smiled?" "Good he said." As he explained that he fell asleep on the beach.

She laughed, as she said, "you are lucky the people who must have seen you asleep may have thought you were a derelict wandering the streets. I promise I won't tell anyone." He said, "would you join me in a quick cup of Angelina's Mexican Coffee?" "Yes, why not, as Angelina heard Deborah's voice, she brought her the special coffee. I will put it on our new menu's."

"He said, "how is the construction going on the new section?" "Great, we are ahead of schedule we are looking at ten days max, unless some unforeseen happens. When the new section is done then the same men will start on the addition to the parsonage. It's an exciting time around the church, the only sad thing that pops up is my Father's indiscretion. He goes to trial in two weeks, he is still out on his own recognizance. He has resolved himself to what is meted out by the jury. God is good, even when we follow the wrong path, he is always ready to forgive." "Amen to that Deborah," said the Preacher. By the way how are things working out for you and Kyle?" "Absolutely fantastic, we are planning on going on a vacation when we find out the outcome of the trial, it will be a family vacation with the boys. Kyle recently received a sizable sum of money from back pay for nine years. We will bless the church and set part of it away for the boy's education. The twins want to visit Yosemite then drive to the Mojave Desert." "He said, "that's wonderful, I'm happy for all of you." Deborah said, "Before I forget, Gil, your friend called us and said that this Saturday he is bringing a puppy, he is a Miniature Dachshund." "I'm so glad you and your family will get a great little dog and fearless, he will fill the void that Little Feller left in their hearts." "Oh, my said Deborah look at the time, I need to help Angelina with food preparation, I'll see you later."

The Preacher finished his coffee and was about to leave when Manny walked into the restaurant and spotted the Preacher. He came over and said to Him, "Preacher, Glad to see you Reverend, this is the first time I have had a chance to see you and thank you for what you did for me. God bless you Reverend, I'm still not sure what I want to be, a doctor or finish college and go into the ministry full time." "When the time comes Manny God will give you the road you must travel. You might consider Medicine first, then the Ministry and then as a Missionary to a Latin country. You will know what your call is." "Thank you Reverend and again thank you for all you have done for me and my family."

The Preacher waved at the two ladies and Manny as he left the restaurant. Perhaps for the last time. As he made his way to the Parsonage as he thanked the Lord for completing his mission. He went up the stairs and into the house. He found Peter and his wife playing on the floor in the living room, with Sarah.

They were startled when he walked in, as they showed a sign of relief on their faces. He told them what happened at the ocean and then having breakfast with Deborah and Angelina. Peter said, "we were worried when you didn't return last night. We went to bed well after midnight, thank God you are alright." "I'm sorry that I caused you pain, but I slept like a newborn babe. I had laid on my back to look at the stars and the moon. The next thing I know; the sun is shining on my face. The sound of the waves hitting the rocks had lulled me to sleep."

"Lydia said, have you had breakfast yet?" "Yes, I have, I had one of the best ever. Angelina fixed one of her specialties, thank you just the same. I was thinking, how would both of you and Sarah like to take a drive to see the Elephant Seals north of here, I haven't seen them myself.

I have been told it is a must. Of course you would have to drive Peter, I'm not sure my klunker can make it, if that's ok with you. I will even buy the gas; besides it is only a few miles up the road." Sarah said, "please Daddy can we go? "Yes, we can sweetheart." Both Peter and Lydia were excited about going as well.

It took about fifteen minutes to get ready, the Preacher had to change clothes shave and they were ready. The Jeremiah's had a 1925 Oldsmobile four door sedan, so they all fit very comfortable. Sarah said, "Daddy do you think we can invite the Johnsen twins?" "We would have to ask their mother, if they can? We'll stop at the restaurant and ask her." They all got into the car, then stopped in front of the restaurant. The Preacher then went inside and soon came back with a smile on his face, and behind him, two young boys came with him, all excited about getting to go see the Seals. They had to wait while Deborah fixed a big bag of sandwiches for everybody to enjoy with soda pop and some cookies.

As they drove away the Preacher sat in the back seat along with the twins. Sarah sat between her mother and daddy. It didn't take very long for them to reach their destination, and to their surprise there were not many cars parked along the road. They all walked on a path of gravel. As they approached the very unstable fence, with a sign posted, that read "Please do not lean on the fence. Sea Lions are very vicious if they feel threatened." The Preacher came over to the boys and Sarah and told them that the Seals are very dangerous, as the males weigh five thousand pounds when fully grown, please don't try to get close by walking on the rocks. They all said that they would be very careful.

They watched the mass of Seals as some cows birthed their babies. The males try to maneuver between the cows and fight other males, to be the Alpha male. Because of their weight, the cows will push them back. It was an exciting time for them all. They decided it was time to eat lunch.

They got back into the car and drove a few miles up the road to a little community with a small grocery store and a little Chapel with picnic tables to sit on, or the lawn. The grass was well watered and was freshly mowed. The smell of clean bright deep green grass shows God's wonderful creation. They chose to sit on the grass and bought some ice from the grocery store, so they could view San Simeon. It was a bright blue clear day, so you could see clear to the top of the millionaire's home San Simeon also called Hearst Castle.

The children wanted to go to the small beach after they had lunch. They all decided to walk down to the beach to help digest their food. The boys and Sarah built a Sand Castle, but not too close to the ocean. After about an hour of building the sand castle the wind picked up and the tide came in with a roar. One of the twins was wading in the outer edge of the water, as a giant wave came in and drenched him along with the other children, but the twin who was in the ocean was caught in a rip tide. The Preacher jumped into the water and with one swoop he grabbed him and swam to shore with the twin hanging onto the Preacher. They were both totally wet, and shivering, but safe.

After this near tragedy, they decided it was time to go home. They walked to the car as Lydia found a couple of towels that they used to dry off. They drove in silence when Peter said: "do you know the song Father Abraham?" "All in unison said yes, let's sing it. Peter said, I'll start the first verse, "Father Abraham had many sons, many sons had Father Abraham, and I am one of them, so let's all praise the Lord." They all sang the first verse, but before you knew it, the children were all asleep.

The Preacher said, "God is so good I thank Him for giving me the strength to do what I had to do. Our children are on loan from God. We are instructed in the Bible to raise them in the discipline of the Lord, the responsibility falls on the father. Christians will give an account to the Lord when we are taken home. Paul writes in Ephesians chapter six that we are responsible for their nurturing in the things of God. They are very fragile when they are young. You only get one chance to raise them according to His word, once they leave the nest then you have no control over their actions."

CHAPTER 18

They pulled in front of the restaurant as the Preacher went inside and found Deborah busy in the kitchen as usual. He told her the whole story. He asked if she wanted him to leave the boys with her or take them to her home where Mother Swensen could bathe them and get them into some dry clothes, she said she would call her mother. He assured Deborah that they were both ok. He went back to the car and asked Peter to drive them home. It was a few blocks from the church. The Preacher along with the twins got out and knocked on the door. He heard a familiar voice say, "I'm coming as she opened the door and said, don't tell me, I can guess what happened, please come in Reverend?" "Mother Swensen, I'm as wet as the boys, so please forgive me, I need to go home and shower and get these stinky clothes off."

He got back into the car as Peter drove to the parsonage. They spent a quiet evening at home. Friday and Saturday was spent relaxing and discussing the works of famous Evangelists and biblical heroes. He shared some of his past experiences that they would encounter, the good and the bad. He asked them if they had mixed feelings about taking over when he was called to another ministry. They asked, "are you leaving right away? We don't know the people and we feel like strangers." The Preacher said, "they want to be loved and treated like you are part of the family. Both of you need to start trusting in God for all your needs, including your emotions."

"You will encounter many nights of sleep disturbance, being called out in the middle of the night for some tragedy. You will learn to know that people are counting on you for comfort in times when a soul is called home. Perhaps a child is in the hospital fighting for his life. A daughter is found with child; how do you comfort the parents. These are the things that you will learn. I'm sure you have experienced some of these in your previous ministry."

When you prepare a sermon, you must remember that you are dealing with people that don't have the scripture knowledge that you do. I have a saying that has helped me over the years, you can only take your congregation as far as you have been in your scripture knowledge, it will help you in guiding your people. Don't be afraid to admit something you don't know. The Holy Spirit will guide you into all truths. I believe that when you reach spiritual maturity you will be a better man. Find an older minister in the area that you can confide in to share with him, as he does with you.

Oh, look at the clock striking ten PM. It's time we all went to bed tomorrow is communion Sunday. Lydia, I know you will be ready to bless us with your voice." They all went to bed and were all sound asleep until six AM.

The sun rose bright and shiny as the blue sky welcomed the first rays of the day. Off in the distance you could hear a rooster crowing, as if to say it's time to get up. The Preacher was the first one to make it to the bathroom. He shaved and took a quick shower, dried off and went into the living room and put on his black suit and his Preacher collar.

He sat in the living room until he heard Lydia rustling in the kitchen making coffee, then she went into the bathroom. He could hear her singing a song, "How Great Thou Art." She had such a mesmerizing beautiful operatic voice. By the time she finished bathing, the coffee was finished perking. He went into the kitchen and poured his coffee into a cup with a healthy portion of canella. He decided to sit on the front porch, which was the home of a warn-out swing. He sat meditating on the Lord. He heard that still voice says, "Leonardo you have done well on this assignment, make sure that you encourage the congregation and I assure you that they will accept Peter and Lydia as their ministers."

He prayed and thanked the Lord for the opportunity

He had given him to put the church in order. His mind drifted to the miracle of Gil's wife when she was healed from a shriveled leg, the ravages of Polio. Perhaps someday they would find a cure or a vaccine for Polio. He prayed to God that he would give an individual the knowledge. He thanked God for sharing this information with him.

He finished his morning prayers. He decided that Peter would bring the message, then he would give a short teaching on gratitude. Perter came out and said, "can I join you Reverend, forgive me for interrupting your prayer time." "No, come sit here with me. I heard your wife singing a gospel song, I heard her the other day, I have never heard such a voice. Let her use her gift to bless the church and perhaps one day she will be able to make a record, then others can hear an angel from God. Who knows, God works in mysterious ways. Peter, I want you to bring the message this morning, I will give a short message on gratitude, after your message."

"Reverend, thank you for the opportunity, I won't let the Lord down. Lydia has made breakfast I don't know if you like biscuits and gravy with eggs on the side." He said, you bet I do, one of my weaknesses is food, I will eat anything that is edible, so let's go. It's eight, o'clock we need to get going."

After they were all ready, they left for the church

and decided to walk. They walked into the church which was jam packed, they had to put a few chairs closer to the pulpit. They opened the service with prayer led by Peter, the Preacher asked Lydia to come forward for her to sing a song. She chose Blessed Assurance, after she finished the congregation was stunned with her voice. They got up and applauded and asked for an encore. She sang The Old Rugged Cross. The Preacher stood up and said, "Reverend Peter will bring the message, please welcome Reverend Peter.

He started his message in the book of Acts, chapter twenty. He spoke on how people reject change, Paul's last visit to Ephesus was a meeting with the elders of the church. The entire chapter stresses encouraging the people, but also to be on guard for the flock. He stressed that unity comes when we place self at the Alter of Grace." He started singing Amazing Grace, and soon his wife Lydia joined him, then the entire congregation began to sing, but even with the entire flock singing, you could hear her voice.

The Preacher stood up and said, "please let us pray and thank God the Holy Spirit for His presence during our time of worship. He looked around and saw men and women weeping, others saying thank you Jesus. He prayed; thank you Heavenly Father for your blessing and assurance that you are real. Paul the Apostle said that we were to give thanks for this is the will of God. Gratitude is being grateful for all that He alone does for us."

The Preacher said a prayer, "thank you Lord for sending me to Cambria, it has been a great blessing and a privilege for me to see what you can do when your sheep love you. I must bid them farewell, as I quote Paul the apostle as he prayed in (Acts 20:36-38KJV) "And when he had thus spoken, he kneeled down, and prayed with them all. As they all wept sore, and fell on Paul's neck, and kissed him, Sorrowing, most of all for the words which he spoke, that they should see his face no more. And they accompanied him unto the ship."

The Preacher stepped down from the pulpit and walked towards the front door. When he got to the front door, the Preacher stepped out into the sunny day with a cool breeze, then turned and faced the congregation, he said good-by to you all as he disappeared.

Epilogue

The people were stunned and sat in their seats as to what happened to the Preacher? They were in agreement that he was an angel, based on some of the things he did in the name of our Lord. He couldn't be anything but an Angel. They were still perplexed at what God had done in their church for the last two months. One of the deacons remembered the letter that was in the desk, he went and retrieved the letter and opened it. On the front of the letter, He had written do not open until I am gone. "Dear board members and congregation; by this time, you have experienced a visitation from the Lord.

You are all wondering if I am an Angel? I was directed by our Lord, to set this church in order, He had been watching the sinful things that some of the members were doing. I will not go into pointing the finger at any individual. All share part of the blame, because the one gift of the Holy Ghost, love was turned aside.

"When you lost sight of what Christ's vision is for His church is love and unity. Our spiritual lives suffer when we neglect praying for unity, as Paul the Apostle in the book of Ephesians, Chapter six. I encouraged Reverend Peter to teach on the gifts of the Spirit. When we replace love for materialism, we unlock the devil and His minions to entice us. Why do you think God destroyed Sodom and Chamorro? Because man replaced faith for a hedonistic life style?"

Our Lord said, (Revelation 3:20-22 (KJV) "Behold, I stand at the door, and knock: if any man hears my voice, and open the door, I will come in to him, and will sup with him, and he with me. To him that overcometh will I grant to sit with me in my throne, even as I also overcame, and am set down with my Father in his throne. He that hath an ear, let him hear what the Spirit saith unto the churches. You lost your first love, You, have repented, and returned to your first love."

I know that you will continue to grow spiritually. You will come together as one. I especially want to thank you all for my acceptance as a man of God. I will never forget you. One more thing; please accept Peter and Lydia along with little Sarah and a new baby that will arrive next spring. They were sent here by our Lord. Farewell with Gods Blessings and Love."

PS, "Am I an Angel, what do you think?"

If you go to Cambria, look for a 1919 Model T Ford, who knows, you may see one, rusting away in a field.

Dedicated to all the men and women who have devoted their lives to sharing the gospel. Men and women who love Christ as I do. Author Dr. Dom Contreras Ph.D.

CPSIA information can be obtained
at www.ICGtesting.com
Printed in the USA
LVHW012149100523
746267LV00006B/23